JIM PENNEY'S GOLDEN NUGGET

JIM PENNEY'S GOLDEN NUGGET

by

Elizabeth Witheridge

illustrated by
Anthony D'Adamo

New York ABINGDON PRESS Nashville

J

Library of Congress Catalog Card Number: 61-5100

TO JIM AND TOM

the boys I know and love best

CONTENTS

JIM PENNEY'S GOLDEN NUGGET

1

AN UNEXPECTED GIFT

"Oh, no!" cried Jim as his old straw hat blew off into the green Monongahela River. He dropped his bamboo pole and string of fish and skidded down the bank after his hat. He landed on all fours in the shallow, muddy water, fish and pole splashing in beside him; but his hat floated lazily away beyond his reach. His fish waggled their tails feebly.

"No, you don't!" shouted Jim. "You don't get away, too!"

Jim grabbed his fish and pole and scrambled up the bank. His face was streaked with mud, and he had torn a three-cornered hole in the shoulder of his shirt. He shook off the water like a wet dog and began to run on the narrow path.

Suddenly the long, wailing whistle of a river boat echoed over the hills. Jim raced faster. It must be the "Monongahela Belle" whistling for the Brownsville landing; it was time for her. The sun had long since crossed the top of the sky. He rounded a bend in the river and there she was, the little stern-wheeler, stopped in the middle of the river. The skiff was ready to take passengers to the dock. It looked like a toy in the distance, and the people getting into it looked like dolls; but they weren't dolls, they were very real. Jim knew all too well that the man stepping into the boat at that moment was his father, Dr. William Penney, and the woman he was lifting down beside him was his bride, Elizabeth Gilbert, Jim's new mother.

Aunt Margaret had warned him to come home early, but the fish were biting. He would never make it now. At least he wouldn't be home in time to clean himself up for the welcome. He estimated the time it would take to row the passengers in from the steamboat, and the time they would need for the short walk up the hill to the parsonage. He looked down at his muddy, bare feet and his ragged pants. If he ran the rest of the way home, he would arrive all out of breath at the very moment his father and stepmother walked into the yard. He could picture everybody's distress at the way he looked. What if he stopped now and waited until all the excitement was over? He could slip in later, probably, without being seen, and get up to the room he shared with his sixteen-year-old brother, Josephus. He could wash up and change his clothes and come down for the homecoming supper. Maybe nobody would think about his being absent. Maybe nobody would.

But deep inside his pounding heart Jim knew exactly what would happen. After the first flurry of greetings and the little cries of happiness from the women, Elizabeth would look around the circle at his little sister Irene in her stiffly starched summer dress, and at Josephus, proper in his Sunday clothes. Her gaze would fall on Aunt Margaret, wearing her second best black silk, and upon Clarissa, who helped in the kitchen. Then she would say, in her warm, friendly voice, "But where is Jim?"

The smile would die out of his father's eyes, and he would turn to Aunt Margaret and say sternly, "Where *is* Jim?"

Aunt Margaret would whisk the silly woman-tears of happiness out of her eyes with her lace-trimmed handkerchief and say, "Why, I can't think whatever could have happened. I told him when he went fishing this morning that he must come home early."

No, there was no good way out. Any way you looked at it, it would be bad, very bad. Jim drew a long breath and plunged ahead. He might as well get it over with. The sooner he got there, the sooner he would know what was going to happen to him for this worst carelessness of all. He was in town now. As he rushed along, his thoughts rushed with him. These same thoughts had filled his mind often since a night some months before.

They were living in Uniontown, twenty miles away,

then. Papa was minister of a little church there, and he also preached in the church at Brownsville, and the tiny new church at Redstone Creek. Besides the preaching, he was a doctor, and many people called him when sickness came to their families. Papa was a very busy man, and so it had been a most unusual treat to have him at home that evening.

"How would you like to move to Brownsville?" he had asked. "The church there has asked me to come to them full time, and I have agreed. Of course, I will still have the church at Redstone Creek, but that won't be hard. It is so near Brownsville. It will be good not to have to ride twenty miles on horseback every time I preach!"

Jim had begun at once to dream of life in Brownsville. The town was on the banks of the Monongahela River. He could fish and swim all summer and skate all winter. He could watch the great towboats on the river, carrying coal down to Pittsburgh. And maybe, just maybe, when he was a little older he would go sailing off on that green river to explore the land that lay on the other side of the hills. The dream had been shattered by his father's voice going on, quicker, and with a touch of excitement in it.

"I will find a house in Brownsville, and after I have moved you there, I am going to bring someone new and wonderful home to be a part of our family." He had cleared his throat and gone on more formally, "Miss Elizabeth Gilbert has consented to become my wife."

Aunt Margaret had begun to sniffle. That was what Jim hated most about women. They always sniffled when they were pleased.

"Oh, William! I am so happy! Such a lovely young woman! And these poor dear children are so in need of a mother."

For once in his life Jim had had enough sense not to say anything, but his mind had raced madly. Poor dear children, indeed! What did they want with a new mother? In the five years since their own mother had died, Aunt Margaret had done very well with them. In fact, from Jim's point of view she had done exceptionally well. When he had done something that Aunt Margaret considered very bad, she would draw herself up to her full black silk height and say, "JAMES, if I were your mother!"

But she wasn't his mother, and by the time Papa arrived home she had usually forgotten about it. Ah, yes, they did very well with Aunt Margaret. Jim could foresee a shocking end to those simple days. Elizabeth Gilbert would be his mother—little Miss Gilbert, his Sunday school teacher in the Uniontown church. Jim shuddered when he thought of the Sabbath mornings when he had sat with the other boys and plotted mischief while she talked. He also shuddered when he remembered the steely look that came into her blue eyes when she thought the plotting had gone far enough.

Well, it was done. They had been married in Union-

town, and Papa had taken her down the river to McKeesport to see his father and mother there. Today he was
bringing her home, and Jim would arrive in disgrace.

At last he was there. He rounded the corner and stumbled into the yard. It was exactly as he had pictured it.
Elizabeth was standing beside his father on the front steps.
She looked very tiny beside the tall thin man in the dark
frock coat. She was smiling and her cheeks were as pink
as the little nosegay of June roses Irene had just given
her. Rene stepped back and made the stiff little curtsey she
had been practicing for days. Elizabeth pulled her close

and kissed the top of her curls, then she looked around and said, just as Jim had imagined, "But where is Jim? Isn't he here?"

Jim was living through a nightmare. Sweat began to run in rivers down the dirt on his face. Suddenly he had an inspiration. He shuffled toward her.

"Here I am," he mumbled. "I have something for you, too."

He held the string of fish out to her. Just at that moment his dog, Fritz, leaped up to welcome him. Jim was thrown completely off balance. He lurched forward, and the wet fish flapped smack against the skirt of Elizabeth's beautiful new traveling gown. Jim raised his eyes in horror as his father's voice broke the silence like the crack of doom, "JAMES!"

The world stood still. Seph clapped his hands to his mouth. Aunt Margaret stood with her handkerchief half-way to her nose. Rene was a little pink statue in her fluffy summer dress. Only Elizabeth moved. She reached out and took the string of fish from Jim's filthy paw. Her eyes were suddenly dancing, but her mouth was perfectly solemn as she said, "My, but you did have good luck, Jim. These are such beauties!"

She held them up to admire, and the sun made a rainbow on their scales.

"Now," she said, "Why don't you clean them? Clarissa will cook them for our supper."

Jim's father opened his mouth to speak, but Elizabeth laid a firm hand on his arm.

"I'd like to go in now, William," she said. He frowned a moment, uncertainly, while Jim's heart nearly stopped, and then his face relaxed. He gave his son a little push toward the backyard, scooped his bride up in his arms and carried her over the threshold. Jim took a firm grip on his fish and fled.

2

GOLD IN CALIFORNIA!

Several days after Papa brought his new wife home, Jim decided to call her "Mother." At first he had addressed her merely as "Say," but he realized that eventually he must call her something. Rene had begun to call her Mama immediately, just as though she had always been in the family. Jim didn't know what Seph would choose to call her. He was away most of the time, working as a deckhand for the summer on Uncle Fred Houghton's towboat. Jim tried "Mama" once. It seemed to fit better with Papa, but he couldn't do it. When he said the word, it brought the picture of his own mother's face too vividly before him. He had been only six when she died, but he could still remember her lovely smile and the sound of her voice.

It wasn't that Jim didn't like Elizabeth, or that he was sorry, really, that Papa had married her. He had thought it was going to be a nuisance, having Elizabeth in the house, but it wasn't. She went around humming little tunes

19

and learning from Clarissa where things were. Clarissa had always been snappish, especially with Jim. She found noisy boys hard to bear, but since the new bride had come, she seemed much more cheerful. Papa was cheerful, too. He kept making excuses to come out of his study when he was working on his sermon and say something to Elizabeth. Jim couldn't remember when he had heard his father whistle, but he whistled often now.

Papa and Elizabeth had been home almost a week when Jim heard the clatter of horses' hoofs on the cobblestones in front of the parsonage.

"Someone's coming," he shouted, racing to the door. "It's your father, and I think he has your trunks," he yelled back. He banged out the door so suddenly that he bumped into the tall, dignified man coming up the walk and almost knocked him down.

"Hold on there, young man. Where are you going in such a hurry?" Harry Gilbert demanded. He gave Jim a friendly little shake and turned him around toward the house. Elizabeth came hurrying out and looked at her father in amazement.

"Why, Papa," she cried, "I had no idea I would see you. I expected Joshua or Corbin would fetch my trunks."

"So did I, daughter," he chuckled dryly, "but your brothers were nowhere to be seen when it was time to set out; so thinking you would probably need these trunks, I decided to drive over myself."

Dr. Penney had now arrived from his study and was shaking hands with the visitor.

"Glad indeed to see you, Father Gilbert," he said cordially. "We'll get these trunks into the house, and Jim can take care of the horses for you."

"I'll help with the trunks," Jim offered eagerly. He could hardly wait to see what was inside of them, and besides, he couldn't bear to miss one word of Mr. Gilbert's conversation. He always told fascinating tales of the travelers who stopped at his inn on the great National Road that ran through Uniontown.

"No, Jim. We can manage the trunks. You take the horses," directed his father.

Jim held his tongue, but he was fuming. The men lifted the heavy trunks out of the wagon and waved Jim on his way.

"Give them water and turn them out to pasture," Papa called after him.

Jim took Molly and Polly down the drive and unhitched them. He pumped water, gave each of them a bucketful, and sent them on their way into the pasture behind the small barn with a slap on their fat grey rumps. Dr. Penney's sleek chestnut riding horse, Spartan, whinnied greetings, and the cow, Daisy, mooed disapprovingly.

Getting back into the house quickly was a problem for Jim. If he went in through the kitchen door, which was the most direct route, he ran the risk of being discovered

and sent to the icehouse to dig a chunk of green Monongahela ice out of the sawdust, or to the well to pump fresh
water for dinner, or on any of a dozen delaying missions.

On the other hand, if he went in by the front door,
Papa was sure to say, "Jim, have you asked Mama if she
needs anything?" Then he would have to go out and see.

If he tried the kitchen door and detoured through the
pantry, he might just be lucky enough to get through without being detained. He decided on the latter course and
was making a run for it when his heel slipped on a wet
spot and he came crashing down. He hit his head on the
corner of a cupboard and cut a gash in his forehead.

"Oh, oh!" he groaned, "Now I'm in for it!"

Elizabeth and Clarissa in the kitchen heard the crash and
the moan and rushed into the pantry. Jim was staggering
to his feet, holding his head. Blood began to drip through
his fingers, and he was a gory sight. Clarissa screamed at
the sight of the blood, but Elizabeth calmly pulled his hand
away from the wound and looked at it.

"I don't really think it's too deep," she reassured him.
"You had better go in and let your father look at it,
though."

Jim could hardly hide his delighted grin as he went into
the parlor. No ice to dig, no water to pump. Dr. Penney
looked at his head.

"Hmm, not bad," he said. "A nice clean cut, and not too
deep. No stitches."

He went off to get some bandages. In a few minutes Jim was all fixed up by his father's skillful hands.

"You look just like a wounded war hero, Jim," Mr. Gilbert assured him. "Lucky your pa's a doctor as well as a minister. Now maybe you'd like to hear a story told me by a fellow stopped at our place yesterday evening."

"That's exactly what I do want to hear, Mr. Gilbert," cried Jim. "I was afraid I'd miss one of your stories!"

"Haven't told a one yet," chuckled Elizabeth's father. "But how does it happen that my new grandson's calling me *Mr.* Gilbert? Can't you find a better name than that for me, boy?"

Harry Gilbert had been a schoolteacher at one time, and Jim stood a little in awe of the tall, rather severe-looking man. Now he flushed and said awkwardly, "Well, sir, I suppose I could call you Grandpa Gilbert. Would that be all right?"

"That would be first rate, Jim," Elizabeth's father replied. "Go ahead."

"Dinner's ready!" called Elizabeth.

It was hot for a day in June, and her hair hung in little damp curls around her face as she came in from the kitchen.

"Dinner's ready," she repeated.

Jim groaned in disappointment. "Grandpa Gilbert was just about to tell one of his stories," he complained. "Who wants to eat?"

"I do," Grandpa Gilbert shot back promptly. "It's a long time since I had breakfast back in Uniontown this morning. Come on, young one, the story will keep."

Dinner seemed endless to Jim that day. It was tedious to hear the grown-up talk about family matters, and even more tiresome to sit through a long political discussion between his father and Grandpa Gilbert. At last it was over, however, and the whole family moved out to the front yard to sit under the trees where it was cooler. Dr. Penney reached into his pocket and pulled out his big silver watch. He looked at it thoughtfully.

"I can only enjoy this distinguished company for a few

minutes," he joked. "Mrs. Smith has sent for me, and I have other calls to make, besides."

"How do you know whether they need you for their souls or their bodies, Doctor?" asked Grandpa Gilbert, chuckling.

Jim's father laughed. "Sometimes I'm not sure which it is, so I take my black bag and my Bible both, to be on the safe side."

Jim couldn't stand it any longer. At the risk of a scolding, he demanded, "Grandpa Gilbert, when *are* you going to tell us the man's story?"

"Oh yes, the story," nodded Harry Gilbert. "Guess I'd better tell it before the doctor gets away."

He stared off across the neighbor's yard while he chewed on a tender end of grass. Jim gritted his teeth and waited.

"Well," he began, "yesterday evening, just as we were getting ready for bed, this man came banging on the door —sailor-fellow, I thought by his rolling walk. Wanted lodging, been walking most of the day. Mother fixed him up with a room, and after breakfast this morning he felt like talking."

Grandpa Gilbert shifted on the soft turf and pulled himself another piece of grass.

"Go on, go on!" urged Jim.

"He'd just come over the mountains from the coast," Harry Gilbert continued. "Shipped into Charleston from around the Horn. Been up to California. You'll never guess what he says is going on out there." He paused a moment, but apparently nobody could guess. "He declares they've found gold in California!"

"Gold in California!" The words seemed to float in the golden sunlight and hover with a drift of white butterflies over the garden. After his first gasp of surprise, Jim sat motionless, lost in dreams. California had fascinated him for months, ever since the United States had taken the territory from Mexico at the close of the Mexican War. It was a magic word whenever it came to his ears. Now the man said there was gold there—gold in California!

Elizabeth's silvery laugh tinkled in the stillness. "But you don't believe it, Papa, do you? Surely this is just one more rumor about California. There have been so many fantastic stories since the war."

Jim was aroused from his dream. "Why not?" he cried. "Why shouldn't we believe it? The man was there. He has just come from California. He ought to know."

Dr. Penney looked thoughtfully at his son. "There are many reasons why we might not believe it, Jim," he said. "The man is a stranger to us. He may be just passing on a tall tale. What do you think, Harry? Did he seem a dependable sort of chap?"

He rose and stood looking down at them, ready to leave on his calls.

"Never would have believed it myself," said Harry Gilbert, "except for this one thing. Now I really don't know."

He put his hand in his pocket. "When he came to leave, he paid me for his lodging and breakfast with this. Tossed it at me as carelessly as if it was a pebble. Said he picked it right out of a rock out there. Here, boy. D'you want it?"

He laid something round and cold and heavy in Jim's hand. Jim stared down at it. He had never seen a gold nugget before; but now, instinctively, he knew that this was one. He held it up to the golden sunlight.

"Is it gold? Is it really *gold?*" he demanded in growing excitement. "Do you mean I may really have it?"

Grandpa Gilbert nodded. "I guess it's gold all right, Jim, and you may have it. It's yours!"

3

HARD TIMES FOR ALL

The golden summer of 1848 rolled on toward autumn all too fast for Jim. All of his old dreams of adventure in the West, and now the new ones of California gold, haunted his waking hours, and his nights, too. Just the lightest touch of the little gold nugget that he carried with him constantly, sent him off to California, across the great plains in a covered wagon, or around the Horn on the pitching deck of a schooner.

"Times are hard," he heard people say all over Brownsville. Jim didn't know exactly what they meant, but he did know that money seemed to be very scarce, and that a great many men were out of work. Half of the great coke ovens that lined the road outside town were shut down. The big towboats had fewer barges of coal to push down through the locks on the river.

Seph was lucky to have his job on Uncle Fred's boat. Most boys his age were loafing around town without anything to do. They gathered in groups at the store and the post office and talked about what they would do when they could get out to California and prospect for gold.

Because "times were hard," the people in Dr. Penney's church didn't have much money, either. Sometimes there was scarcely any in the collection plates on Sunday morning. After a Sunday like that Jim's father stopped whistling, and Elizabeth went about her work with a worried line between her eyes. They seldom talked about their money worries where Jim could hear, but one morning he came upon them after he finished his chores. Dr. Penney was sitting at his big, old desk in the study, with his new sermon half finished in front of him.

Jim stuck his head in to ask if he could go fishing just in time to hear his father say sadly, "My dear, I never should have asked you to marry me!"

Jim was so shocked that he forgot about going fishing. "Why *not?*" he broke in. "I think everything is working out fine."

They both jumped, and then they began to laugh.

"I think things are working out fine, too, Jim," Elizabeth assured him. "Papa didn't mean he was sorry he married me. He just meant that the church people haven't been able to pay him very much lately, and he is afraid it bothers me. It doesn't. He needn't worry about that."

Jim looked anxiously at his father. "Does it mean we don't have any money?" he asked.

His fingers found the little gold nugget in his pocket and tightened around it. His quick eyes caught the glance that passed between his father and mother.

"That's what it does mean," he cried. "I can tell by the way you're looking at each other. Here, take this."

He laid the little shining gold nugget down on the desk in front of his father. Elizabeth covered her face with her hands and wept. Never in his life had Jim seen a grown person cry, except Aunt Margaret when she was happy. He felt a dreadful churning pain in his stomach.

"What's the matter with her?" he begged his father. "What did I do? I didn't mean to!"

Elizabeth reached out for him blindly. "Of course you didn't do anything," she sobbed. "I'm crying because I think that's the most generous thing I ever heard of, and I'm crying because a child has to be worried over money matters."

"I'm not a child," declared Jim indignantly.

Dr. Penney cleared his throat and walked over to the window for a moment. When he came back, he pulled Jim over to him.

"All right, son," he said, "you're not a child. I don't believe a child could have given up a thing so precious to him as that nugget is to you. You have a right to know what is troubling your mother and me."

He sat down at his desk again, and Jim stood beside him.

"You see, Jim," his father began, "even in good times,

ministers don't make very much money. We have to de-
pend upon the money that the members put in the collection plate at meetings. The Brownsville church and the
church at Redstone Creek between them promised to pay
me four hundred dollars for a year's work. Times are so
hard this year that they haven't been able to pay that much,
so, of course, it has been hard for us to pay our bills. Winter will be here before we know it, and we need money for
coal. You and Rene will need new shoes for school——"
His voice trailed off, and Jim saw a discouraged look slide
over his face.

"You get paid for doctoring, though. People pay you for that, don't they?" Jim asked quickly.

He had never thought seriously of these things before. His father came and went constantly, busy about his work day and night, preaching and helping people. Jim had never heard him complain. Suddenly hot, red shame welled up inside of him. He had never stopped to think before how hard it might be to get the money that put the food on the table and the shoes on his feet. Dr. Penney reached into his desk and pulled out a big ledger. He riffled through the pages that were covered with lists of names.

"These are the people I have been 'doctoring,' Jim, as you put it," he said. "Some of them have paid me, but most of them haven't for quite a long time. Times are very hard."

"I think that's awful!" Jim exploded. His dark eyes flashed, and he threw back his shaggy head angrily. "Why do you do it, if they don't pay you? What do they think you do it for, anyhow?"

"I suppose they think I do it because I want to help them," his father said quietly. "Would you want me to say, 'Can you pay me? If you can't, I won't take care of your sick baby'?" His dark grey eyes gazed steadily into Jim's brown ones. Jim turned his head away.

"We-e-ll," he muttered, "I guess not, but I don't think it's right."

"Shall I refuse to preach next Sabbath because there may

not be enough money in the offering to pay my salary?" Dr. Penney pressed.

Jim scowled and kicked at the rag carpet with his bare toe. "No, I guess not."

His father stood up, and Jim felt dismissed. "You take your nugget back, Jim," Dr. Penney said. He held out the bit of gold, and his eyes lit up with a smile. "It was fine of you to offer it, but you must keep it yourself. We will manage."

"No!" cried Jim, violently. "I want you to keep it. Then you will have it if you need it. I won't take it back!"

He set his mouth in hard, stubborn lines. Dr. Penney stood looking at his son thoughtfully. He tossed the shining little nugget up and down gently in his long, thin hand. Then his face relaxed and he said, "All right, Jimmy. I'll keep it, but I will never use it. I shall keep it until the day comes that you need it for something very important in your life. Perhaps that will be the day when you go away to college to start training for what you want to be."

"College!" Jim almost shouted the word at his father. "I will never go to college. I don't want to be educated. Look at what education has done for you! All it got you is two jobs that you don't get paid for. No, sir! I don't want to be a doctor or a minister. Some day I will take my nugget and go out West and make a lot of money for all of us. You don't have to have an education to make a lot of money. No, sir!"

Dr. Penney started to say something, then he changed his mind and turned to his desk. He dropped the nugget into a little drawer and sat down to the unfinished sermon. Elizabeth gave a little sigh and reached out to push the hair back from Jim's hot forehead.

"You go on down to the river and catch us some of those nice big fish for dinner," she said.

4

DANNY STOPS OFF

It was autumn when Danny came to Brownsville, and gold lay thick on the Pennsylvania hills. Jim had rushed down to the river right after school. It was too cold to swim, but he had brought his pole along. He had just stuck a worm on the hook when he looked up directly into Danny's green eyes.

Jim blinked. "Who are you?" he demanded.

Danny accepted the question as an invitation and sat down beside Jim on a stone.

"I'm Danny," he announced. "Danny Higgins."

Jim blinked again. His first impression of Danny was rather dazzling. The afternoon sun glinted on the boy's red hair and pointed up the bright brown freckles on his round face. Jim stared, and then turned to watch his pole, dipping in the green river. He jerked the line, and up came a fish. Jim took it off the hook, put on another worm, and tossed the line back in. Then he turned to Danny again.

"I'm Jim Penney," he said, introducing himself. "You're new around here, huh?"

Danny nodded and crossed one patched knee over the other. The boys sat in silence for a few minutes. Jim fished and watched the boats going down the river. Suddenly Danny shouted, and pointed to a clumsy flatboat drifting on the green current near their side.

"There," he cried, "that's the kind of boat my pa's agoing to make for us!"

Jim watched the awkward thing floating along. It had a little cabin in the middle, and children and animals were scattered around its crude deck.

"They're probably going down the Ohio as far as they can go, and then overland to California," he said wistfully. "People have been going down the Monongahela most of the summer, ever since the news came about the gold out West. I fish and watch them go by."

"That's where we're agoing," Danny declared excitedly. "We're agoing out to Californy to get gold. We'll be on our way soon's Pa gets the boat built, and the baby comes."

Jim looked at Danny with respect. So this boy with the patched pants was going to California.

"Why doesn't he get the men at the shipyard to build your boat?" he asked. "If he builds it all alone, it will take so long that you'll never get on the river this fall. The river will freeze up pretty soon, and then you'll have to wait until spring."

Danny nodded soberly. "Yeah, I know. But Pa doesn't have much money. He has to build our boat himself. We're going to have a new baby, too. I've got two sisters already —hope this one's a boy. Ma doesn't want to travel on the river with a new baby. I 'spose we'll have to stay here all winter."

He stared out at the water forlornly.

Jim felt sorry for Danny. "Where will you stay?" he asked.

"I don't know," said Danny. "We just got here. We come over the mountains with our horse and wagon from the East. Pa's fixing to put up the tent now. Probably I better go see if he needs me. Want to come along and meet my folks?"

Jim was delighted. He pulled in his line, with a fish on it that had gone unnoticed while they talked, and walked along the river with Danny. The tent was up, and Jim saw the little sisters playing around in the dirt in front of it. The father was chopping firewood. Mrs. Higgins was fixing something to eat in a huge iron kettle over an open fire. This reminded Jim that it was nearly dinnertime, so after he was introduced to the family, he ran home to see what was cooking for his own supper.

Over the eggs and fried potatoes that night, he told

about Danny and the others. Elizabeth sighed and shook her head at the thought of a new baby in a tent.

"We'll have to do something about that, William," she said in distress.

"I'm afraid they won't be the only ones in hard straits this winter," Dr. Penney answered heavily. "There doesn't seem to be any let-up in the stream of people coming over the mountain. The ice won't hold off forever. Some of them are bound to be caught along the river and have to stay the winter."

At this point Seph took up the conversation. "Better not get too chummy with this Danny, Jim," he warned. "You don't know anything about him. Some mighty funny folks have gone down the river this summer."

"So?" Jim flared at him. "You don't know anything about Danny's family, either. I've seen them, and they're nice. Danny is going to be here all winter, and I 'spose he will go to school. He's going to be my friend. So, Mr. Josephus Penney!"

Jim slammed out of the room, leaving his dish of applesauce untouched. He stuck his head back in the door and said, " 'Scuse me," and then began to count his way up the steep, narrow stairs to his room, his and Seph's. Darkness came early now, and the younger ones, Rene and Jim, weren't allowed to carry candles upstairs as a general practice. One, two, three, four——he heard Seph laugh, the kind of grown up, superior laugh that always made Jim so furious. Then Papa's voice followed, quiet and low.

"All right," answered Seph, "but he's so——"

Jim missed the rest of the sentence. Nine, ten——he was at the landing now. Twelve, thirteen——he was in the upper hall and across it into the dimness of his room. There wasn't a moon, but there was skyshine beyond the open window, and Jim's eyes, so used to the velvet dark, could see far.

It was very warm for late autumn. He sat down on the floor beside the open window and rested his head on the sill. It felt cool and good, and he was close to the stars that hung low over the town. Houses clung to the hillside below the parsonage, and Jim could see over their rooftops to the meetinghouse, with its pointed gable against the sky.

His river ran close; he could hear it near him. And he could see the lanterns on a towboat, sparkling through the trees like fireflies. It was going down to Pittsburgh, down to the place where the Monongahela and the Allegheny flowed together to make the great Ohio River. Danny was going there some day. The crazy flatboat that his father would build was going to carry red-haired Danny to Pittsburgh and far beyond, off where the mark of the sun still lingered in the sky.

Everybody was going; everybody, that is, except Jim. The big boys who talked about it on corners this summer had gone. The people from the other side of the mountains had climbed into boats from the shipyards and floated away. Next spring, when the ice went out of the Monongahela, Danny and his family would float away from him, too; he would be left alone on the banks of his river to catch fish for supper. He squeezed his eyes tight to contain the tears. He must have slept.

Suddenly Seph was shaking him and hissing in his ear, "It's time to go to bed, boy."

Jim was up with the sun the next morning. He had business. He raced through his chores before breakfast, chores that usually took him forever. Clarissa gasped at the speed with which the kitchen woodbox was filled. He pumped a bucket of water furiously and splashed it all over the kitchen on his way in. Clarissa's protesting wails were drowned by the scrape of his chair as he slid into his seat at the breakfast table.

It was unusually hard for Jim to bear the long blessing. His first spoonful of oatmeal was on its way to his mouth before Papa's last word died away.

"What's the rush?" inquired Seph, placidly pouring milk on his porridge.

"I'm going to take Danny to school with me this morning," Jim announced.

"Huh!" observed Seph, "Don't be surprised if he doesn't go. My experience with these gold chasers is that they aren't much interested in education. All they can think of is getting out to California."

Jim struggled to hang onto his temper. "What's the matter with that, I'd like to know?" he demanded, his mouth full of cornbread. "Every fellow I know, except you, has gone already. Why don't *you* go? Just tell me that."

"I'm not interested," replied Seph loftily.

"No, you're 'not interested,' " Jim mocked. "All you're interested in is riding up and down the river in Uncle Fred's towboat. Oh, if I had your chance I'd be off on the river. But I'd go someplace on the river. The Mononga-hela doesn't just turn around at Pittsburgh and come back, you know. I'd be off on the big river, on a keelboat, or maybe even a steamer!"

"Well, I must confess I might be interested in going West with Papa next spring," said Seph, thoughtfully. "But I certainly wouldn't want to stay."

Jim choked on his oatmeal.

"West with Papa? Next spring!"

His eyes leaped frantically to his father's face.

"Are you really going West, Papa?" he cried. "Are you going to California? Nobody told me!"

Dr. Penney smiled. "Nobody told you, Jim, because we didn't want you to get excited. Spring is a long way off. Many things can happen before the time comes. No, I'm not going to California. Just going West, maybe as far as Iowa, on church business."

"Seph isn't really going, is he?" pleaded Jim. "You're just saying that to tease me, aren't you? I'm the one who wants to go West. I always have. *I'm* the one!"

42

Dr. Penney's eyes grew serious. "You forget," he answered, "that Seph is much older than you are. If he can raise the money for his fare, I expect he will go."

Jim subsided. He knew he would gain nothing by arguing when Papa looked like that, but he had to grit his teeth and clench his fists under the table to keep the furious tears back. In a few minutes he left the table silently and started out for the riverbank and Danny, but all the light had gone out of the morning for him.

5

WHY NOT GO?

"Come 'ere, Jim. Be quick!" Danny commanded.

He had been waiting for Jim in the schoolyard one morning early in November. The two went over to a private spot away from the other boys where they could talk alone.

"A couple boys stopped at our camp last night. They're agoing downriver on a raft all by themselves. They're on their way West. Ma gave 'em supper, and afterwards we went outside and talked."

He paused a moment for breath, and Jim urged him on.

"Hurry up, Dan, the bell's going to ring in a minute. What about it?"

"Well," Danny continued, looking over his shoulder to make sure they weren't being overheard, "they aren't agoing to wait until spring. They're agoing to go right on as far as they can before the river freezes up. Maybe they'll get as far as Kentucky and stop there. They say we're

44

crazy to wait until spring. All the gold will be gone by the time we get to Californy. I told them about the baby, so they said why don't I go with them."

Several boys they knew walked by, and Danny waited until they were safely out of earshot.

"I told 'em I had a friend was crazy to go, too; and they said put our clothes in a blanket and go along with 'em, both of us. I'm agoing, Jim."

Jim caught his breath. His mind was in a whirl. The whole idea had caught him completely off guard.

"Why, I couldn't go, Danny," he said. "Papa would never let me. He'd say I was too young."

"Don't ask him!" Danny exclaimed urgently. "I'm not agoing to ask Pa. He won't care after he sees all the gold I get out there. No siree! I'm not agoing to ask anybody, not me. I'll roll up some extry clothes in a blanket and be off with the fellows before sunup tomorrow. Come on, Jim. You'll be sorry all the rest of your life if you don't."

"I have to think," Jim said, pondering. "A fellow can't just go off. Besides, I haven't any money."

The school bell jangled through the early morning air, and Jim and Danny reluctantly started toward the door.

"You've got your nugget," Danny whispered softly. "Didn't your pa say it was to be kept for something *big* in your life?"

"Yeah, he did say that," Jim agreed.

"Well?" prodded Danny.

There was no time for further talk. The things that Danny had said kept boiling in Jim's mind all day. He couldn't even recite. The schoolmaster finally rapped his knuckles sharply in sheer exasperation. But at last he knew what he would do. He'd go; it would serve them all right for keeping Papa's trip West a secret from him, and for planning to let Seph go instead of him. He'd go; they'd forgive him when he came home again with hundreds of thousands of nuggets like the one in Papa's desk. He would be the one in the family who could pay the bills when the church people and Papa's patients didn't pay him. He'd go; what if he was only eleven? He was almost twelve. Even Papa had admitted he wasn't a child anymore.

After school that night, he and Danny walked down toward the tent on the banks of the river. Jim had made up his mind and he should have felt terribly excited, but he didn't. All he felt was a kind of cold heaviness. He decided this was probably because it had all happend in such a hurry. There hadn't been time to straighten everything out in his mind. Later he would feel gay and elated. Now he had to decide what to take and how to manage all the details of getting away.

"I'll go, Danny," he finally said, in a rather small voice.

Danny showed all the excitement that Jim lacked. He was wild. His voice rose higher and higher and suddenly he burst out with the parody on the Stephen Foster song that everybody had been singing all summer:

"I'm going to California,
  The gold dust for to see!
I'm going to California
  With my washbowl on my knee!"

"Are you crazy, Dan?" hissed Jim. "Somebody will hear you. "Come on, if we're going tomorrow morning we've got to plan now."

They had just begun to make serious plans when they saw Dr. Penney walking beside the river ahead of them. His head was bent in thought. He often called on the people who had built a little temporary village on the banks of the Monongahela, those people who had come over the mountains too late to get on the river before winter set in. They were living in tents and rude shacks and anything else they could find to give them shelter. Jim knew that his father was deeply concerned about them as the cold weather approached.

Dr. Penny stopped to speak to Danny's father, who was working on their flatboat, and then disappeared into the tent where Mrs. Higgins was. The boys stopped outside, and Danny whispered, "I'll come up tonight after supper, and we'll plan some more."

Jim nodded. In a moment his father came out of the tent with a worried frown on his face, and Jim walked toward home with him.

"I must talk to your mother about that poor woman," he

47

said, sighing deeply. "I can't think what will become of her in that tent when the baby arrives. It will be very soon now, too."

"Mmm," murmured Jim absently.

His mind was on other things. When he got home, he would do the chores just as usual, as if nothing were any different. When he had a good chance, he would slip into the study unobserved to get the nugget out of the desk. Suddenly he realized that neither of them had said anything for quite a time. He glanced quickly at Papa to see if he could possibly suspect that anything was wrong. But Dr. Penney was walking along absently with a troubled look on his face, his eyes on the far hills.

They were going up the parsonage path now, and Rene popped out of the bushes where she had been hiding. Papa tossed her to his shoulder and hurried into the house. Jim loitered through the door. It was warm inside, and sweet with the smell of fresh bread in the oven. His mouth watered. There would be hot bread for supper.

It was candlelighting, and Seph had pulled a chair close to the candelabra on the sitting room table and was reading, as usual. Elizabeth came in from the kitchen with her face flushed and a streak of flour across her small nose.

"We're having fresh bread for supper, as you can probably smell," she announced gaily. "It will be ready pretty soon. It must be cold outdoors, William. Don't you think we had better have a fire in here?"

Jim watched his father light the fire. The dry kindling caught and flames began to crackle up the chimney. Jim went to the window and stared out into the thickening darkness. Clouds were rolling across the sky, covering the stars. The wind began to rise and whistle around the windows of the old house with a whisper of the coming cold.

Jim shivered and turned back to the bright warmth of the sitting room. Then he climbed the steep, dark stairs slowly to change his clothes for chores. The chores seemed endless. Spartan was restless, and Daisy was crosser than usual. At last he was through in the barn. He carried the bucket of warm milk in to Clarissa and went out to pump water for supper. When he came into the kitchen again, he could hear the family talking in the sitting room.

This was the time to get the nugget; now, before he looked out again at the cold dark. He needed to feel its solid weight in his hand. When he had the nugget snugly nested in his pocket, he was sure he would feel the confidence that had made him say to Danny, "I'll go."

Jim slipped out of the bright kitchen down the shadowy hall to the study. He crept over to the desk and pulled out the little drawer where Papa had dropped the nugget. His fingers explored the things in it. There were several pieces of paper, a pen, a penwiper, and the nugget. It had slid down under everything. Just as Jim touched it a great gust of wind swirled around the house and wailed in the chimney. He clutched the nugget and pushed it into his pocket; then he ran out of the room, back to the candlelight and the firelight in the sitting room.

"Supper!" called Elizabeth.

Everybody hurried to the table. Elizabeth poured cups of tea, and Papa ladled vegetable soup into bowls. Jim looked around the table, remembering that this might be the last time he would see them all at supper for a long time. They sat there so unsuspectingly, eating from the familiar blue and white dishes. Rene bit off a piece of crust on her back teeth because her front teeth were out, and crunched noisily.

"Chew with your mouth closed, Rene," reminded Elizabeth gently.

The wind wailed again in the chimney. Jim shivered uncontrollably, and Dr. Penney glanced at him quickly.

"What's the trouble, son?" he asked. "You haven't eaten a thing. Not even your bread."

Jim looked down at his plate. It was true. He hadn't even tasted the wonderful bread. Another shiver seized him. Papa was waiting for an explanation.

"Oh, I guess I don't feel very good," mumbled Jim.

Elizabeth reached over and felt his forehead. "He's hot, William," she said anxiously. "I believe he's having chills and fever. He probably took cold when the weather changed so suddenly this afternoon."

"Perhaps so," said Papa absently. "He'd better go to

bed right after supper. Right now my mind's on that poor woman down on the riverbank in the tent. A storm's blowing up, and her baby's due any minute."

Elizabeth was instantly all concerned for Mrs. Higgins. Jim was delighted that everybody's attention was diverted to something else. At least it would give him time to think. Although it nearly choked him, he forced himself to eat a slice of bread and gulp down some milk.

It would be dreadful if Papa remembered what he had said and made him go to bed right after supper. He and Danny had to be together to plan. He had to get a blanket and all his warm clothes, and figure out some way to get out of the house without waking Seph or anybody else. His biggest problem would be to slip away in the predawn darkness without disturbing Fritz. The dog slept in the barn and went off like a firecracker if he heard the slightest sound in the night.

The wind moaned in the chimney again, and Seph went to put another log on the fire. Rene wriggled with joy.

"Oh, I love it like this!" she purred. "I love the fire and the candles and the wind outside and all of us here together."

An awful pain began in Jim's stomach. He squeezed the nugget in his pocket for comfort, but it didn't work. Suddently he saw a picture in his mind of the family tomorrow night. He would be off somewhere on the river, looking a long, long way ahead to sunny California.

"I'm going to California,
The gold dust for to see!"

The gay song echoed and re-echoed in his head, but now it didn't sound as happy as it had this afternoon when Danny sang it on the riverbank. It sang itself to the sad tune of the wailing wind in the chimney. Dr. Penney stood up and that was the signal for everyone to leave the table. It was Rene's turn to wipe the dishes for Clarissa tonight. Jim could slip away. He counted his way up to the stair landing in the dark, and there he sat down for a minute to think.

"Jim," called Papa, "Jim! You had better go up to bed now."

Jim groaned. Just then the sound of the front-door knocker hammered through the house over the whishing of the wind with a kind of frightening urgency. "That's Danny!" Jim thought. He clattered down the stairs, but not in time to keep Seph from opening the door. It *was* Danny. Jim heard his voice, but he wasn't asking for Jim.

"Is the Doc here?" he cried breathlessly, as though he had been running all the way in the wind. "My pa sent me for him. Ma isn't feeling good."

Jim rushed into the sitting room. Elizabeth hurried in from the kitchen with Rene at her heels. Papa was already putting on his heavy coat and giving orders.

"Danny, go back to the river and bring your little sisters

52

up here. Your family can stay with us. The rest of you remain here so I'll know where to get you if need be."

He picked up his bag and started for the door, but Elizabeth stopped him. She was pulling her heavy winter shawl tight around her.

"I'm going with you, William," she said. "You'll need me there. And we'll bring her straight to the parsonage as soon as possible. I should have seen to it long before this."

"You are to stay here, Elizabeth," Papa said firmly. "I'll need you more right here. You and the children get the spare room warm and ready, and you can take charge when I bring her home."

With that he picked up his bag and disappeared into the cold darkness.

Danny's little brother was born that night in the tent on the banks of the stormy Monongahela. Dr. Penney brought him home to the parsonage, with his mother and father.

"I haven't got much money, Doc," Mr. Higgins said, "but we'll be everlastingly grateful to you for what you did for us tonight. I'd like to name the young 'un after you. What do you say, Ma?"

Mrs. Higgins cuddled her baby close to her as she lay in the big, warm spare-room bed. Her eyes were bright with tears.

"William Penney Higgins, that's what it will be," she nodded, "William Penney Higgins!"

It was late that night before all the Penneys and all the Higginses were bedded down and the parsonage candles were snuffed out. After the excitement of the new baby, Jim's mind reverted to the big boys who were going West at the break of dawn. Danny was sleeping with him and Jim tried to get his attention several times. But Danny seemed strangely disinterested, for one who had been so excited just a few short hours before. All he seemed to think about was "Willie," as he had already begun to call his small brother.

Finally Jim gave up and turned over. He was very sleepy, and every time a blast of wind shook the old house, he burrowed deeper under the covers. In a few minutes sleep had erased all thought of a trip on the rolling green river.

The next time Jim opened his eyes, the cold white light of dawn was pushing through the shutters. He poked Danny.

"Hey," he whispered, "those fellows must be getting ready to go. It's sunup."

"Who cares?" yawned Danny, rolling over and pulling the quilts off Jim.

"I do!" answered Jim. "But I'm too sleepy to do anything about it now."

He rolled over the other way and pulled the quilts back again.

6

HOPE AT LAST

Jim had so much fun while Danny was living at the parsonage that he would have liked to keep the family there forever. But Mr. and Mrs. Higgins insisted that they must leave as soon as the baby was old enough to move safely.

"You're not going to live in that tent this winter!" cried Elizabeth, cuddling the baby in her arms.

"Pa hasn't got enough money to rent a house," answered Mrs. Higgins sadly. "So I don't know what else we can do."

"I'll find you a place to live," Jim assured her. "Just wait."

And he did find a place. It was a log cabin in the woods back of the Sharpless Paper Mill near the Redstone Creek Church.

"Sure the Higginses can live there, Jim," agreed Mr. Sharpless, owner of the mill, when Jim asked him about it after church one Sabbath morning. "Last tenant was a man who worked for me in the mill. Left for California last summer. As a matter of fact, I've been thinking of hiring me a new man. If Higgins is steady and wants a job, I'd like to talk to him."

There was no question about Mr. Higgins wanting the job. Just before the first real snow of the winter, he moved his family out to Redstone Creek and Jim was left behind in a parsonage grown suddenly very dull.

One evening, early in December, when Papa was out and Jim was prowling restlessly around the room instead of doing his arithmetic, Seph looked up from his book and said casually, "I saw Uncle Fred today, Mama."

"Oh?" said Elizabeth, putting down the sock she was darning, "He was here in Brownsville, then?"

"Yes," nodded Seph, "just up for an hour or two, seeing about the new towboat they're building for him over at the shipyard. Didn't have time to come over to the house. Mama, you can't imagine what he asked me!"

Seph put down his book and began to pace the floor, too. His usually sober grey eyes were sparkling.

"He asked me if I'd like to be assistant to the pilot of the new boat next summer if——"

"Bully for you!" interrupted Jim.

He rushed over and thumped his brother on the back.

Seph scowled at Jim. "Just a minute," he said, waving his hand. "I said IF, you remember. Uncle Fred said he'd like to have me IF Caleb Jones goes out to California as he's talking of doing now. Caleb's been waiting two summers to get into the pilot house, so it wouldn't be fair to put me over him if he still wants the job."

"Of course not," agreed Elizabeth. "But I do hope it works out for you, Seph. Wouldn't it be fine?"

"You'd learn to steer the boat!" cried Jim.

He began to dream, picturing his brother at the wheel of the glistening new towboat, shoving the huge coal barges down the Monongahela. Suddenly his heart jolted as a new idea came to him.

"Seph!" he cried, "if you get the towboat job, you couldn't go West with Papa, could you?"

"I don't suppose so," said Seph. "I'd hate missing the trip, but do you realize what that job would mean to me, Mama?"

He turned to Elizabeth and paid no more attention to his excited brother.

"But Seph," Jim insisted, "how can you bear to think of giving up the trip? You could probably go on the towboat another summer. This may be the last chance you'll have to go out West. If I were the one, I'd give up anything in the world to go with Papa!"

"I know you would," Seph agreed impatiently, "but I'm not a bit like you, remember. I have plans for my future."

"Oh, I have, too!" cried Jim. "I have, too."

He was hopping around the room now. His black eyes were sparkling with excitement.

"My plans don't include staying cooped up in the hills of western Pennsylvania all the rest of my life. I don't intend to spend my life toting coal from West Virginia down to Pittsburgh with a towboat. No siree! I'm going down the river and see what's on the other side of the hills. I'm going to be the one in the family to have adventures."

"Oh," said Elizabeth, quietly, "I thought maybe you were going to be the one in the family to follow your father in medicine or the ministry."

Jim stopped hopping. "*Me?*" he snorted in astonishment. "*Me* be a doctor or a minister? I should say not. Whatever made you think that?"

"Because you have such a lot of energy," said Elizabeth. "And you like people."

"I like people all right," agreed Jim. "But I don't like people who expect Papa to preach to them and take care of them and then never pay him for it. No, ma'am! I don't like people that well."

Elizabeth picked up her mending again and made no comment. Jim went to the front window and stared moodily out into the snowy darkness.

"Papa's coming down the road," he reported.

Elizabeth jumped up from her rocking chair. "Seph, put another log on the fire. Papa will be cold," she said.

"Jim, get his slippers. I'll fix a cup of tea. You go to bed, Rene. It's way past your bedtime."

She hurried out to the kitchen, and Rene slowly picked up her dolls. Dr. Penney was stamping his feet on the front porch, and in a moment he was in the warm, candle-lit room. Rene raced to fling herself into his arms.

"Why, Rene!" he cried. "What are you doing up at this hour? Here, wait a minute until I get this wet coat off. It has started to snow again."

He set her on the floor and pulled his heavy coat off.

"Let me take it," said Elizabeth, arriving from the kitchen. "Rene is up because nobody remembered to send her to bed. Hurry along now, sister."

"Please let me stay up just a minute and listen to Papa," begged Rene.

"Just a minute, then," agreed Papa.

He sat down in his big chair before the fire and she sat on the rug nearby. Jim came to stand in front of him.

"Do you know why nobody remembered to send her to bed?" he began. "It was because we were having the most exciting conversation. Seph is going to get a new job this summer, Papa."

"Now just a minute," interrupted Seph. "We don't know whether I'm going to get the job or not, and besides, this is my story, not yours."

"What's this, Seph?" demanded Dr. Penney. "Let's hear about it."

So Seph came to sit beside his father at the hearth and tell his story. Jim sat on the rug and leaned against Papa's knee. Elizabeth pulled up her rocker to listen. Beyond the walls of the old house the snow-laden wind rushed by, and the candles wavered in the draft that crept in around the windows.

"I won't know for sure until Caleb makes up his mind," Seph finished. "It may be nearly spring before I know."

Jim got up on his knees and swiveled to face his father.

"Seph can't go West with you if he goes on the river," he stated. His black eyes searched Papa's face as he spoke.

"I don't suppose he can," Dr. Penney agreed.

Jim waited in agony for his father to say the thing he longed to hear. There was no sound in the room except the whispering of the wind and the faint sizzling of a green log in the fireplace. Elizabeth rocked gently, and her chair creaked. Rene's eyes drooped shut as she snuggled closer to the fire. Jim couldn't stand it any longer.

"Papa!" he cried, and his voice was loud and sharp in the stillness. "You know what I mean. Can I go? Can I go West with you if Seph gets his job?"

"You!" exclaimed Dr. Penney. "Why, you're only——"

He hesitated and Jim thought he was going to say, "you're only a child." The furious red sprang to his face, but Papa went on carefully.

"You're only eleven years old, and I don't see how you would be able to raise the money for your expenses. Seph has saved some money and planned to earn more to pay his own way. We don't have money enough to let you have it from the family purse. You haven't saved any money, Jim, have you? It burns a hole in your pocket, somehow!"

Jim was on his feet now. His heart was pounding so hard he thought everybody in the room must hear it.

"I'll earn the money," he shouted. "I can, and I will save it. You just wait and see!"

Rene roused and whimpered.

"Mercy, Jim! You've frightened the child," said Elizabeth. "No more of this talk tonight. You have to go to school in the morning. Off to bed with you. Take Rene and go upstairs."

Jim's eyes flashed, but he mumbled his goodnights and took his sleepy little sister by the hand. As he counted their way up the dark stairs, he heard his mother say softly, "Well, William, what do you think?"

Most of his father's reply was lost, but he heard his last words, "I really don't know what to say. He's such a head-over-heels fellow."

7

CHRISTMAS SURPRISES

Snow came early to the hills that year. Not two days after Seph's startling announcement, it snowed very hard. One of the neighbors hailed Jim after school and asked him to shovel the paths and do the evening chores. He himself was ill with a cold. Afterward he tossed Jim a dime.

Jime rushed home with the precious coin and showed it to Elizabeth.

"You keep it," he said to her. "It is the beginning of my money for the trip West with Papa."

"I'll tell you what we had better do with it, Jim," she said. "You get down that old, cracked sugar bowl from the top shelf in the kitchen and you can keep your Western money in it."

The little piece of money tinkled lonesomely in the bottom of the big, blue sugar bowl, but it was a beginning. Soon there would be many more to keep it company, Jim promised himself.

Nobody talked about the thing that was in Jim's mind day in and day out. Nobody asked him how his fund was coming, but one day Elizabeth found ten cents that she had lost a long time before and gave it to him.

"Put it in your sugar bowl, Jim," she said. So then Jim knew that she was thinking about it, too.

The thought in Jim's mind constantly, from the moment he opened his eyes in the morning until he closed them at night, was, "What will the trip West cost? How much money do I have to earn?"

The fund in the old sugar bowl grew. It grew slowly, but finally when Jim counted it there was a dollar rattling around in the depths. He was afraid to ask his father how much money he would need. He was afraid to know, and he couldn't bear not to know. One day not long before Christmas, when there were two dollars in the bowl, he screwed up his courage and asked. Papa had just come home from a preaching trip that had kept him away for more than a week. He was sitting before the fire, warming his feet. Suddenly he held out his hand and said, "Come here, Jim."

Jim settled on the arm of Papa's chair and waited.

Papa cleared his throat. "Mama tells me," he began, "that you have been very busy while I was away and that, in addition, you have behaved yourself pretty well. She tells me that you have nearly run your feet off doing errands for everybody in town who would let you."

65

"Yes, sir," Jim replied. A wide grin spread over his face.

"And what, may I inquire, is the occasion for all this errand-running?" Dr. Penney asked, with a twinkle in his grey eyes.

Jim controlled his desire to shout, "You know!" and answered politely.

"I'm trying to save money, Papa."

"Indeed!" exclaimed his father. "A most commendable pastime!"

He dropped his teasing manner and said seriously, "Jim, are you still counting on the trip West next spring?"

"Oh, yes," cried Jim. "I am earning every penny I can, and I put it in my sugar bowl. I have two dollars now."

It was hard to keep the quiver out of his voice, but he rushed on before he lost his courage.

"How much will it cost, Papa? How much will I have to earn?"

Dr. Penney looked soberly at his son.

"I'm not sure," he said slowly. "For me the fare will be about thirty-five dollars, there and back. Then I shall have to plan for some extra expenses—food and lodging in places where we have no friends or relatives. I shall have to have at least fifty dollars to be safe. It would probably be less for a boy. It might not cost more than twenty-five dollars."

Not more than twenty-five dollars! Jim felt as if someone had struck him right in the middle. His father might as well have said twenty-five hundred dollars. He sat perfectly still, fighting for command of himself. He hadn't felt so much like crying since he was a little boy. He couldn't cry now. He was eleven, almost twelve. He didn't cry in front of anyone, not even his own father. Jim had the feeling, too, that if he acted like a little boy, Papa would be more than ever convinced that he was far too young to take along on a trip West. He pulled himself up out of his gloomy thoughts in time to hear his father go on.

"And the money isn't all of it, Jim. I do not feel at all sure that you are old enough to make this trip with me, even if Seph doesn't go. Your mother's report on your behavior was good this time, but there have been occassions when I have been away from home that her letters were full of your misdeeds, and she has been in despair of your ever growing up."

Papa put his fingers under Jim's chin and tipped his drooping head up, so that he could see his eyes. For a long moment the grey eyes and the brown eyes looked steadily into each other. It was the brown eyes that shifted first.

"I know," muttered Jim, "but I'm going to be different from now on. I'm going to earn the money, and I'm going to act like a man. You'll see, Papa."

Dr. Penney's stern face relaxed, and he gave Jim a friendly poke.

"All right, son, we'll see," he said. "Now, go and do your chores."

Christmas came, and the parsonage was full of quiet excitement. There was never great feasting and celebrating in the minister's family. In the church it was a quiet time of gratitude for the coming of the Christ Child. Jim's family exchanged little gifts among themselves, though, and the children went around whispering secrets and making things behind closed doors. Rene made lumpy little pincushions, and Jim made calendars and penwipers. Elizabeth was busy, too. She spent hours alone, finishing the gifts she was knitting for everyone. There was a bright blue hood for Rene, warm socks for Seph, and a handsome gray wool muffler for Papa. Jim supposed she was knitting something for him, too. Somehow she even found time to knit a white bonnet for William Penney Higgins' first Christmas.

Grandmother and Grandfather Penney were coming up from McKeesport for a visit, and Elizabeth was busy getting the house in shining order for them. The day before Christmas it was Jim's responsibility to lay the fire in the spare room. He piled the kindling and logs in neatly, gave a quick final brush to the hearth, and lit the fire with coals he carried from the kitchen stove. He ran downstairs into the Christmas Eve twilight. There the spicy smell of mince pies baking in the kitchen mingled with applewood burning in the fireplace.

He heard the silver sound of Elizabeth's laugh followed by Rene's high-pitched giggle, and almost immediately the chime of sleigh bells in the street. Jim rushed to the door. Grandfather and Grandmother were there in the cutter, all bundled up in fur robes. They had driven up the river on the ice from McKeesport, and they were cold and hungry.

That evening after supper they all sat beside the fire to open the small presents they had for each other. The gifts were piled on the old wooden settle and covered with Elizabeth's best black shawl. Because Rene was the youngest member of the family, she was allowed to distribute them. They were opened one at a time, while everyone else watched and waited.

By the time the pile of presents under the shawl was gone, almost everybody in the room was decked out in new finery. Jim had a fine jackknife from Seph, and one of Rene's lumpy pincushions; but he had nothing from Papa or the grandparents, and nothing from Elizabeth. He had been so sure she was knitting something for him, too.

Suddenly Dr. Penney leaned forward and cleared his throat.

"Rene," he said, and his eyes were twinkling, "Are you perfectly sure there weren't any more presents under the shawl? I thought there was something else for Jim."

"I don't think so," she assured him, "but I'll look again."

She rummaged underneath the folds of the big shawl.

"Here!" she cried, pulling out a small parcel. "Is this it? It says 'Jim' on it."

Jim snatched the package from her and began to tear it open. All the talk in the room had stopped, and everyone was watching him. There was Elizabeth's gift—a pair of dark blue knitted gloves, with long, bright red cuffs. They felt uncommonly heavy, and they made a sort of noise as he laid them down on his knees. A puzzled frown crinkled Jim's forehead. Suddenly everyone in the room began to laugh. Elizabeth finally wiped her eyes and spoke up.

"Oh, Jim, you look so funny! Try them on and see if they fit."

Jim put his right hand into the glove and shouted in wild excitement, "Hey! There's something in here!"

He took the glove and tipped it upside down on the floor. Money rolled out of every finger. Money from Papa and Elizabeth, from Grandmother and Grandfather, from Seph, and even a half dime that Rene had earned for him. Hastily he shook out the other glove—more money. Grandfather Gilbert had written from Uniontown saying to put in a dollar and he would pay it back the next time he drove over to Brownsville. Aunt Margaret had sent money from McKeesport, and Clarissa had slipped a ten cent piece into the little finger before she had gone home for Christmas. Last of all something wrapped up in a scrap of paper fell out. When Jim opened it, he found three big round pennies and a note on the bit of paper:

"Dear Jim,
    I hop ya git to go West.
        Yer frend,
            Dan"

In a sort of daze Jim began to pick the money up from the floor. Then he snapped wide awake and raced for the blue sugar bowl on the top shelf of the cupboard. The hum of conversation began again in the room, while Rene and Jim sat down on the hearth rug to count the money. Three dollars and ninety-five cents, and he hadn't had to earn one cent of it! Then he took out the money already in the sugar bowl. He had worked hard the past few weeks, after he had learned how much he would need. There was five dollars in change already in the bowl. Altogether he had $8.95. It began to look like a lot of money. He put it all carefully back into the bowl and went to sit on the arm of his father's chair.

The family stopped talking to hear the announcement of his wealth.

"It's about a third, isn't it, Papa?" Jim stated, rather than asked. "When I get the other two-thirds, I can go."

Dr. Penney laughed and squeezed Jim's knee. "I'm glad you have the money, boy," he said, "but when you get the rest of it you will still have just one-third of what it takes to go. Another third is Seph's job on the boat, and the most important third of all is your behavior the rest of the winter!"

8

JIM'S TRAGIC LOSS

"James, if this ever happens again you shall be soundly thrashed and I shall take the matter to your father."

The thunder of the schoolmaster's voice and the sharp crack of his ruler on Jim's knuckles sounded together in the sudden stillness of the schoolroom. He had been drawing pictures of steamboats on his slate when he should have been doing sums. His heart pounded miserably. The last thing in the world he wanted at this point was to have any trouble reported to Papa. Jim remembered all too well what Dr. Penney had said on Christmas Eve: "Most important of all is your behavior the rest of the winter!"

Rene's curls drooped studiously over her slate, but Jim knew right well that she was taking in every one of the master's words. Would she tell at home? He suffered through the rest of the afternoon somehow and hurried home alone. The house was perfectly quiet. Papa was out making calls and Elizabeth was having tea with Hannah

Binns. Clarissa wasn't at home either. It was her day out.

Jim knew he should go out right away and do his chores. But he was still stinging from the master's ruler and his sharp rebuke. It was nice being alone in the house for awhile. It would be a good chance to get his money down from the shelf and count it in private. There had been nearly ten dollars in the sugar bowl the last time he figured it up.

Jim reached up and felt for the bowl in the familiar place. The cupboard shelf was bare. The old blue sugar bowl, holding all of Jim's money, was gone. Frantically he swept his hand along the shelf. No, it hadn't just been moved out of its usual place. It was gone.

Jim stood in stunned silence. The back door opened as he emerged from his state of shock, and Rene came into the room. He darted at her.

"Where's my money?" he demanded.

He grabbed her by the shoulders and emphasized each word with a shake.

"Your money?" cried Rene indignantly. "How should I know? Isn't it on the top shelf where you always put it?"

Jim shook her again. "No it isn't on the top shelf. Where did you put it?"

She twisted away from him. "You leave me alone, Jim Penney! If you touch me again, I'll tell Papa what happened in school today."

Jim was scarlet with rage. "You tell Papa what happened, and I'll tell him you stole my money, you tattle-tale, you!"

He was so angry that he didn't hear the door open again and Elizabeth's footsteps behind him.

"Jim!" she exclaimed. "What in the world is going on here?"

Rene ran to her mother and whimpered into her skirts. Jim shrugged his shoulders in contempt.

"Girls!" he muttered scornfully. "They always have to cry. I didn't do anything to her, just asked her if she knew where my money was."

"He did, too," said Rene. "He shook me and said I stole his money."

Elizabeth sat down on the stool and said, "All right, Jim. I want the story."

He told her and finished sheepishly, "I don't suppose Rene did take it, but if she didn't who did? It's gone."

"Did you ask Clarissa?" suggested Elizabeth.

"No," said Jim, "she's gone, too."

"Of course, it's her day out." Elizabeth recalled something more. "She cleaned the kitchen before she went. I expect she put your sugar bowl someplace else, Jim."

Jim was pacing up and down the floor. "That's all very well," he cried, "but it doesn't get my money back. Do you realize what this means? If I lose my money, I can't go out West with Papa."

"Why all the commotion?" demanded Dr. Penney, coming in the back door at that moment. "Daisy's bawling, Jim. Why aren't you doing your chores?"

Jim had to tell the story all over again, and he did it with a warning eye on Rene.

"Mmm," murmured Dr. Penney with a twinkle in his eye, "there's been a rumor around town that a robber was spotted over in Uniontown last night. They think he headed for Brownsville. Maybe he took your money."

"I'll bet he did," cried Jim. "I'll bet that's it. The door was unlocked, and everybody was away. He got in and took my money!"

"Quiet, boy," soothed his father. "I was only joking. What would a robber be looking for in a poor minister's parsonage?"

Jim subsided, but he was only half convinced.

"Let's look for the sugar bowl," Elizabeth suggested sensibly.

They searched the house, all four of them until Papa gave up and went into his study to read and Elizabeth had to stop so that she could cook supper. Jim went out unhappily to do the chores. When Elizabeth called him to supper, he couldn't eat. Not a trace of his money had been found. More and more Jim was leaning to the theory that the robber had been there and stolen it.

While he and Rene were washing the dishes after supper, Clarissa arrived.

" 'Course I know where the sugar bowl is," she responded to Jim's question. "When I was cleaning the cupboard this afternon, I came across it and thought to myself that I'd better not leave it there, what with robbers around and all; so I hid it."

"For goodness sakes, where?" cried Jim. "We've looked all over."

Clarissa chuckled. "Hid it good, didn't I?"

She led Jim upstairs to her room. She reached in under the quilts and feather bed and extracted his precious sugar bowl.

Jim rushed downstairs with it and announced in a loud voice, "This settles it. I'm not going to trust my money to the sugar bowl any longer. I'm going to keep it with me day and night after this."

"That is the best way I can think of to lose it," said Seph, who had come home in the meantime. "You start carrying it around in your pocket and you'll lose it for sure."

"Seph's right, Jim," agreed Papa. "It's safer at home than any other place."

Jim set his mouth in stubborn lines and began to count his money. It was all there, of course, all $9.52½ worth of it.

"I'm going to make a bag for it," said Jim firmly.

He borrowed Elizabeth's needle and found some black cloth in her piece box. By bedtime he had awkwardly sewed a small, fat pouch with a drawstring in the top. He transferred the money to it carefully and put it under his pillow that night.

It began to snow in the night, and when Jim looked out early in the morning it was still coming down in great, soft, furry flakes. He shoveled a narrow path so that he could do the chores, and later plowed through waist-deep drifts to school. Rene was kept at home that day.

It snowed steadily all day. School was let out early and Jim plowed over to earn a few pennies shoveling for old Mr. Smith who had rheumatism. He pulled the fat little bag of coins from his pocket and tucked the pennies into it. Then he went home to milk Daisy. When the chores were done, he went off to slide down the long hill with the boys.

Many boys had homemade sleds, but others, lacking them, pressed anything at hand into service. Jim had an old board, slick and smooth from much skimming down the hill. He threw himself on his stomach on the board and whizzed away between the huge drifts. Over and over he swooped down the slope, until he was too tired to climb up again.

The snow had almost stopped and there was a trace of sunset in the west when Jim started home.

"Fight! Fight!" somebody yelled in the twilight. Ahead of him Jim could see a half-dozen boys standing in a circle. In the middle of it two of his friends were rolling in the snow, locked in noisy combat. Just as Jim arrived, a big fellow, known to everyone as the school bully, jumped into the ring and began to pound the smaller of the boys. Jim couldn't stand it; he dropped his board and waded in. The bully left the small boy and turned on Jim. He picked him up by the back of his jacket and hurled him into a snowdrift. Jim swam out, sputtering and wiping snow from his eyes and nose. He attacked with all the fury of a bull terrier.

Over and over the boys rolled in the drifts. Jim's jacket was torn and his nose was bloody. One eye was beginning to close with a dark purple bruise. The other boys had stopped fighting and stood watching. There was no sound but the rasping sound of heavy breathing and the yells of encouragement for Jim. He was beginning to wonder how much longer he could keep going with the big fellow when Seph came walking along on his way home for supper. The fight ended with startling suddenness. The bully melted away into the snowy darkness and the rest of the boys set off for home. Seph picked Jim out of a snowdrift and surveyed the damage.

"Let's go home," he growled. "Looks as though you got the worst of it. What makes you pick fights with fellows twice your size?"

"I did not," Jim started to sputter indignantly, and then he put his hand into his pocket to feel for the fat little money bag.

"Seph, it's gone!" His voice was a wail in the dimness.

"What's gone?"

Seph was striding on ahead of him through the drifts.

"My money. It's gone. I had it after school. I put some pennies from Mr. Smith in it and put it back in my pocket."

Seph stopped walking. "All right. Stop and think where you've been."

"Well," said Jim reluctantly, "I did my chores and then I went coasting on the long hill."

"You idiot!" exclaimed Seph. "Do you mean to stand there and tell me that you went coasting with all that money in your pocket?"

Jim hung his head. "Uh huh," he said dejectedly. "Will you help me look, Seph?"

"Well, I'll help you," said Seph, "but it will be like looking for a needle in a haystack in all these drifts. Did you have it when you left the hill to come home?"

"I don't know," replied Jim miserably. "All I know is that I had it when I went to the hill."

"Huh!" grunted Seph. "Then you might have dropped it where you were fighting, or back on the hill, or anywhere in between."

"I suppose so," Jim agreed.

They looked first in the trampled snow where the boys had been scuffling. Jim crawled around on his hands and knees, sifting the soft snow between his fingers.

"I guess it isn't here," he admitted finally. "Let's go over to the hill."

The early dark had fallen over the snow, but the moon was showing through ragged clouds. It was well past supper time, but Jim had forgotten all about eating. Seph's long legs carried him swiftly through the drifts, and Jim trudged along behind him, his eyes on the snow. The drifts were as soft and fluffy as a feather bed and as he walked Jim became increasingly convinced that his money bag must have gone to the bottom of one of them.

"I won't find it until spring," he moaned, but he began to search the long slope doggedly.

"Maybe somebody found it and took it home," suggested Seph in a clumsy attempt to cheer him up.

Jim brightened momentarily. "Maybe," he cried, because he wanted so intensely to believe it. "I'll ask at school tomorrow." But he felt quite sure that nobody had.

"Well, let's go home, boy," Seph said finally, with a kind of rough sympathy in his voice. "I'm starving."

"I'm not," said Jim, "but I s'pose we might as well stop looking for tonight. I'm cold."

During the whole long nightmare of an evening not one person said, "I told you so." After the first shock, each member of the family went about his affairs in sympathetic silence. Finally Papa looked at the big silver watch and said, "Bedtime, children."

Rene said timidly, "I suppose you will have to start earning your money all over again, won't you Jim? I'll help you."

"All over again?" echoed Jim, bitterly.

He stared at her with smarting eyes. "Oh, sure! In just a few days I can save almost ten dollars. It will be real easy!"

He stumbled upstairs, pulled off his clothes in the cold blackness, and crawled despairingly into bed.

9

CAT AND MOUSE

The next few days weren't so bad. They were almost fun, because Jim was the center of attention both at home and at school. Everybody dug through the drifts on the long hill and sifted the snow at the scene of the fight. Even the schoolmaster expressed sympathy, and the bully lumbered around through the drifts, helping, too. Jim felt a kind of pleasant excitement each time he walked into school and the whisper went over the room, "Have you found it yet?"

Jim's mind refused to accept the fact that the money might be lost permanently in the snow. He was so sure that somewhere under the deep white cover someone's probing fingers would touch the fat little bag. Everybody had his own theory as to what had happened. Danny came down to help look, and he even suggested that maybe the robber found it and made off with it.

"He's s'posed to be around here somewhere, you know."

"No, Dan," said Jim wearily, "I guess it just must have fallen into a drift and it'll stay there until next spring, if I ever do find it at all."

The January days ran swiftly along and still there was no trace of the money bag. Jim's friends forgot to ask daily if he had found it and spent their after-school hours sledding on the long hill or skating on the river. At home Elizabeth busied herself knitting long, warm stockings for her family. Sometimes she looked anxiously at Jim over the flashing steel needles, for now he sat silently in the house after his evening chores were finished.

He couldn't bear to go sliding on the long hill because all of his dreams of adventure were buried somewhere along that trail. He wanted to forget about it as soon as he could, and when he went out to skate or to coast it all came back with dreadful sharpness. It was easier to sit in the house and shut his mind off. That way he felt comfortably numb.

One day Jonathan Binns asked Jim to deliver a telegram. It was such a marvelous new invention that ordinarily he would have been wildly excited at the chance, but now he went stolidly. Later Mr. Binns handed him a half-dime for the errand and peered over his spectacles at him curiously.

"Heard that you lost quite a sum of money a spell back, Jim," he said. "What you going to do with this? Start your new savings?"

"Oh, no!" Jim said, eyeing the coin sadly, "I guess I'm all through with that, sir. You see, I couldn't possibly save enough money now to go West when Papa goes in the spring."

Johnathan Binns snorted. "Humph, I never did hold with youngsters going West. You're needed right here. What d'you suppose we're going to do for a doctor and a parson when your pa gets too old to work? You better be thinking about saving money for an education, young one. It takes education, these days. You can't just watch somebody else do it and then go out and do it yourself anymore. No siree, you got to get an education, boy!"

Jim nodded politely, thanked him, and went off home. Strange that people kept talking to him about being a doctor or a minister. Just a little while ago it had been Elizabeth and now it was Mr. Binns. Everybody knew Jim was set on adventure out West. Why did they even think of anything else? Well, they could just forget about it. He had no intention of following a career that kept a man working day and night for almost nothing.

When he brought the milk into the kitchen that evening, he stood looking at the cupboard thoughtfully and then he reached up and felt for the old blue sugar bowl on the top shelf. It was still there. Without comment he dropped the little half-dime into its emptiness and set it back on the shelf.

After that night Jim felt better. It was a winter of unusually heavy snow, and quite often he was asked to shovel for people who for some reason couldn't do their own shoveling. The pennies he was given chimed down into the depths of the blue sugar bowl. Grandpa Gilbert heard of Jim's catastrophe and sent a half dollar in a letter to Elizabeth. Jim wouldn't have believed such generosity could exist, and it was at that point he dared let himself begin to dream again. It was a slight, frail dream, but there was hope, because by the middle of February there were two dollars in the sugar bowl.

Not only did the snowy winter mean shoveling for Jim to do, but it was indirectly the means of his working out another money-raising project. The schoolmaster was in trouble, serious trouble. There were mice in the school-house. They came in through holes in the old frame building because the snow was so deep that they couldn't find food outside. Mice were everywhere. They gnawed holes in lunch baskets and nibbled the food. When girls found the little grey beasties in their lunch baskets at noon, they screamed, and no amount of threatening by the schoolmaster hushed them. Threats of the ruler or even the strap failed to keep the girls from climbing on benches when the mice scampered across the schoolroom during classes. Let just one mouse show his whiskers, and as one girl they all clutched their skirts and leaped to the benches while the boys roared with delight.

Discipline was breaking down. The schoolmaster was

frantic. He tried plugging up the holes, but the mice got in anyhow. He tried setting traps, but they ate the cheese and played leap frog with them. The mouse that ran boldly up Rene's stocking and hid in the lace on her pantalettes was the last straw. Rene started a long, ear-splitting scream and held it until some of the big girls rushed her into the cloakroom and located the creature. Then they all screamed.

The schoolmaster stood up in back of his high desk and gazed sternly down upon his pupils. An expectant hush settled over the room. Rene came in, looking pale and frightened. Jim wondered if his little sister was going to be whipped for the shriek. He couldn't blame her for doing it, funny as it seemed to a boy. The master was silent as he looked around, and the loud ticking of the clock could be heard in the room. He cleared his throat.

"Something must be done," he intoned. "These rodents must go. I will pay the sum of," he hesitated for a moment, "one dollar to the person who can get rid of them for me."

One whole dollar! A gasp went over the room, followed by stunned silence. Jim's hand went up.

"I'll get rid of them for you, sir," he cried eagerly. "I've a plan. All you have to do is to let everybody stay after school. We'll take care of the mice."

Thirty children gathered around Jim at the front of the room that afternoon.

"What we need is cats," he explained, "all the cats we

can get. Now you all go home and see if you can get a cat. Bring 'em back here after supper tonight, and I'll take care of the rest. Run along now, all of you."

The little ones started to go, anxious to be off on the cat hunt, but some of the older ones stayed, and a murmur of dissatisfaction rose in the room.

"That's all right for you, Jim," one of the boys said. "You get the dollar, and we do the work."

"It isn't fair!" several voices began.

Jim reddened. "Well, maybe it isn't," he conceded reluctantly. He made a quick decision. "Tell you what. I'll pay you a penny for every cat you bring to the schoolhouse, and I get the rest of the dollar. Fair enough? After all, it was my idea!"

Everyone agreed, and they all separated to round up the cats. Jim borrowed the schoolhouse key from the master and went on his way home whistling. He hadn't felt so gay since he lost his money. Tomorrow there would be lots more money for the blue sugar bowl. Even after he had paid off the ones who brought cats, there should be at least seventy cents left for him. Maybe some of the big ones would bring more than one cat; but on the other hand, chances were good that lots of the little ones wouldn't bring any at all.

At the supper table that night Rene told about her terrifying experience with the mouse, and Jim related his plan for getting rid of the pests.

"It's a good idea," Papa agreed, "but I don't think you can count on much money for your travel fund."

"I should say not," Seph chimed in with his most exasperating grin. "All the cats in Brownsville will be there."

"You just wait and see," Jim answered confidently.

The family said no more. Jim and Rene went out to the barn to dig old Tabby out of her snug nest in the haymow and carry her down to the schoolhouse. The sky was crystal clear that night, and the moon was full. Jim could see his friends hurrying down the steep roads, converging on the schoolhouse. Tabby began to yowl in protest, and she was answered by dozens of anguished meows. They made quite a parade. The white light from the moon shone down upon tiger cats, black cats, yellow cats, white cats, soft grey tabbies, battle-scarred old Toms, long-haired aristocrats, mothy-looking alley cats.

Jim unlocked the door of the schoolhouse, and the cats poured in. One of the girls stood at the door and kept track of the number on her slate. Finally all of them seemed to have arrived, so Jim, nursing two deep scratches on his hands and one across his nose, locked the door. He and Rene began the climb back up the hill to the parsonage.

"My goodness," chattered Rene, running along beside Jim, "did you ever see so many cats? I bet every cat in Brownsville is there, just as Seph said. Do you suppose they'll fight with each other all night, Jim? Maybe there won't be anything left of them in the morning!"

"I hope they concentrate on the mice," laughed Jim. "All I hope is that there isn't anything left of the mice in the morning."

"How many cats came?" Elizabeth wanted to know when they walked into the house.

"Lots," sighed Jim. "I'll bet there are seventy cents worth of cats in that schoolhouse right now. Mary Anne kept track of them for me on her slate."

"Too bad," Elizabeth sympathized, "you certainly could have done with fewer cats! How do you suppose they are all getting on together, shut up in that small space?"

Jim had to grin in spite of himself. "I don't know," he admitted. "Some of them were spitting and hissing at each other when I left."

Jim was at school the next morning before the master. He opened the door cautiously and peered in. The cats were distributed about the room in various positions. Some of them were washing their faces on the window sills in the early morning sunlight; some of them were curled up together to keep warm. He noticed that several of them had new scratches across their noses and one or two old veterans had freshly scalloped ears.

When they saw Jim, they arose and stretched and

yawned. With great dignity they strolled toward the door, and when the schoolmaster walked up the path he met seventy-odd cats walking down. He and Jim began a search of the building, but not a trace of a mouse was to be seen.

"You've done well, James," the schoolmaster congratulated. "It was a good plan. Now we'll have a peaceful, quiet day with no interruptions."

He handed Jim a cloth bag, heavy with coins. "I've brought your money in pennies," he said, "for I heard that you are paying a penny for each cat."

Jim groaned. "That's right, sir," he said, "and Mary Anne said there were seventy-two cats!"

When the pupils came to school a little while later, Jim was at the door to pay them off. School began. No nibbling noises came from the cloakroom; no mice scampered across the floor; no girls screamed. The schoolmaster beamed down upon them benignly. Blessed silence prevailed. The only sound in the room was the scratching of slate pencils and the mumbling of the second grade reading class.

Suddenly the stillness was shattered by a shrill feminine squeal, "There's Polly's cat, and she's got a mouse in her mouth!"

All eyes were riveted on the cloakroom door. Without a doubt it was Polly's striped yellow cat, Goldilocks, coming into the room with something in her mouth.

"It's a mouse!" screamed the girls, preparing to take to the benches again.

The schoolmaster rapped in vain for order. He took off his spectacles and glared down upon Goldilocks.

"It isn't a mouse!" cried Jim. "It's a kitten!"

The girls began to giggle. The boys joined in with loud guffaws, and even the schoolmaster's face relaxed into a sort of half-smile. Goldilocks paraded proudly across the room and laid her kitten gently down on the floor beside the glowing coal stove. She dashed back into the cold, dark cloakroom and returned in a minute with another kitten in her mouth. She made the trip over and over while the whole school watched, fascinated. At final count there were six kittens in a furry heap beside the stove.

The schoolmaster found a box for the kittens, and Polly lifted each one tenderly in while Goldilocks looked on, making anxious, motherly noises. On the way back to her seat, Polly stopped beside Jim and held out her hand, palm up.

"Six more pennies," she demanded.

"Six more pennies?" he cried. "Those kittens didn't catch any mice!"

"You promised a penny for each cat," Polly insisted stoutly, "and I have seven cats here."

For the second time that morning the schoolroom was in chaos and even the schoolmaster laughed at the look on Jim's face.

"Pay up, Jim! Pay up! She's got seven cats here. She's right. You owe her six more pennies!" everybody shouted.

Jim's face was red, but he painfully drew his few remaining coins from his pocket and counted out six. Polly said, "Thank you," dropped him a saucy little curtsey and walked demurely to her seat. The schoolmaster rapped for order, and Jim began to do a problem in arithmetic on his slate. He set the figures down ruefully:

$$100 \qquad 28$$
$$-72 \qquad -6$$
$$\overline{} \qquad \overline{}$$
$$28 \qquad 22$$

10

THIEF IN THE NIGHT

"Why don't you look for Si Thompson's pig and claim the reward, Jim?" asked Danny one mild day in the early part of March.

Jim was helping Danny sweep out the mill that morning. He had been working for Mr. Sharpless on Saturdays for several weeks. Mr. Sharpless had come to see him one day when he was in town and offered him five dollars if he wanted to help Danny around the mill on Saturdays from then until May. Jim was delighted. It was a wonderful opportunity to earn real money, and he and Danny had a chance to be together again.

This particular Saturday Jim was feeling low in his mind. The night before he had counted the money in the sugar bowl for the first time in a week or so and it was discouraging. He had only $3.56.

"Even with the five dollars from Mr. Sharpless in May," he told Danny, "I probably won't have more than $14.00

or so, no matter how hard I work. It takes so long to earn a dollar."

"Well," said Danny thoughtfully, "warn't you sort of figgerin' on stayin' out there with your relations, anyhow, and goin' farther West when you git a chance? Fourteen dollars would be enough to go one way."

"Ssh!" hissed Jim, looking around hastily, "don't say it out loud, Dan. That's a secret between you and me. 'Course I want to stay out there; but Papa doesn't know that, and he'd never let me start out without money enough to bring me back."

"Better go lookin' for that pig, then," observed Danny.

"How much is the reward?" asked Jim curiously.

He swept the dirt out the door and sat down to rest.

"I don't know," said Danny, "but it must be quite a sum. A pig's real valuable, and Si set enough store by this one to put a notice in the paper. Pa read it out this mornin'."

"Wonder where a fella'd start looking," pondered Jim.

"Thompson's place is across the creek and t'other side of the big woods," volunteered Danny. "Pa thinks probably the pig got lost in the woods."

"Better start looking there, then," said Jim. "Tell you what, Dan. I'm going to stay all night with you tonight and ride home with Papa after he preaches tomorrow. After we get through work tonight, let's you and me go out looking for that pig."

Danny hesitated. "Aw, come on," Jim coaxed. "I'll split the reward with you," he offered handsomely.

A funny look came over Danny's face. "The more I think of it," he began slowly, "the more I guess maybe you and me had better not go into that woods after all, Jim."

"Not go into the woods?" cried Jim. "Are you crazy, Danny? What's there to be afraid of in the woods?"

"I don't know for sure," answered Danny, reddening under Jim's ridicule, "but I think there's something. Funny things have been goin' on around here lately."

"What funny things?" asked Jim. "Let's hear about it."

"Well," began Danny reluctantly, "ever since the time that robber was reported in Uniontown, funny things have been goin' on. Like once I saw smoke in the woods, as though somebody had a fire, and one night I saw a light, sure as anything, movin' around."

"That all?" asked Jim sceptically. "You must have been reading some dime novels, Dan!"

"I have not!" flared Danny. "And that isn't all, Mr. Smarty. Mr. Sharpless has been missing chickens lately and the other evenin', come milking time, his black cow, Bessie, was missing, too. She never come home until mornin' and she'd been *milked!*"

He stopped and waited for Jim's reaction. "Now, Dan," protested Jim, laughing, "do you expect me to believe that?"

"I guess I should know," declared Danny, "I'm the one who milks her. Go ahead and laugh, Jim. Pa laughed, too, but Mr. Sharpless didn't laugh. He even said that he'd give a reward to anybody who found out who was taking his chickens and milking his cow."

"Who do you think has been doing it?" Jim asked, with a grin still showing at the corners of his mouth.

"I think it's that robber from Uniontown," said Danny firmly. "I think he's holed up in the woods over across the creek, and he's stealing chickens and milk to live on."

"Hmm," mused Jim, forgetting his amusement, "maybe he stole Si Thompson's pig. Maybe the pig isn't lost. We better go look for that pig, Danny."

"Would you go into that woods, knowing what I just told you?" demanded Danny.

"Of course," said Jim boldly. "It's still light when we get through work. Let's go poking around a little and see what we can find. We can always run if we see anybody."

Danny shivered with excitement. "All right," he agreed, "but I don't think it's smart."

Late that afternoon Jim and Danny went into the woods. In the deep woods there was still snow in spite of the thaw. The boys plunged into drifts up to their knees sometimes, and Jim went into an oozy bog over his boot-tops. They plowed ahead, pushing undergrowth aside and calling warily, "oink, oink," imagining they might get an answering "oink" from Si Thompson's pig.

All was silent in the woods, a threatening kind of silence, Jim thought privately. They crossed the creek cautiously on swelling ice, and suddenly broke through a heavy thicket of scrub trees into a small clearing. It was almost dark now, but enough light filtered through so that they could see a dilapidated log hut. There were no windows in the building and there was no sign of life around it, but there were footprints in the soggy snow. From a nearby tree there hung the plump, skinned carcass of some animal.

The boys ducked back into the shelter of the trees.

"Si Thompson's pig!" exclaimed Jim under his breath, with a little thrill of fear running up his spine.

"Looks like a pig all right," agreed Danny. "Where do you 'spose the feller is? Maybe he's inside."

"Maybe," nodded Jim. "Think I'll go have a look."

"You will not!" cried Danny, forgetting to be guarded. "We're going home right now and tell Pa and Mr. Sharpless."

Jim gave in. "All right," he said, "I won't go inside; but we aren't going to tell your father and Mr. Sharpless yet. We'll come back again and try to round up the fellow. We don't know for sure that it's the robber. Maybe somebody just lives here."

"Nobody just lives here," objected Danny. "Mr. Sharpless says nobody lives between the creek and Thompson's."

"All right," said Jim, "but we'll come back, anyhow."

That night something happened that put the whole thing temporarily out of Jim's mind. It began to rain, and the time that Jim had been long awaiting was at hand. The warm, late-winter rain would wash away the remaining snowbanks on the long hill. Now Jim could search every inch of it for the fat little black bag with his money inside.

It rained all the Sabbath day. Jim rode home with his father in the buggy after meeting. As soon as they were in Brownsville, he raced out through the rain to look at the hill. The stubborn drifts still hung on in spite of the pouring rain.

When he went to school the next morning, it was still raining and at last the remaining hard-packed snow was honey-combed. Jim felt sure that during the day it would disappear. After school he made himself wait until chores were done and supper was over before he began the search. He said nothing of his plans at home. For some reason that he couldn't put into words, he wanted to do this alone. Perhaps it was because he couldn't bear to have anyone see his terrible disappointment if he didn't find his money bag.

The rain had ended and it was clearing around the edges of the sky. A last trace of sun illumined the long hill as Jim reached its top. His eyes swept down the slope, following the course his board had taken that fatal day in January when the fat black bag disappeared. Midway down the hill, outlined in gold by the setting sun, lay a fat, round object. It could be a stone, of course, but Jim knew it wasn't. It was his bag, his money bag. All these cold weeks it had lain there, hidden safely by the concealing snow.

Jim gave a wild, triumphant shout and started to race toward it when suddenly he realized that he was not alone on the hill, that there was movement in the bushes beside the sled trail, opposite the little black bag. Involuntarily he slackened his pace, and in that brief instant a large, dark figure darted out of the underbrush and swooped up the precious bag. The man ran heavily down the hill with Jim leaping frantically after him, yelling, "That's mine! Stop thief! Stop, help! help!"

Nobody was there to hear Jim's anguished cries. It was candlelighting and the streets of Brownsville were de-

101

serted. The thief ran on, dashing around corners and ducking between trees and buildings, until Jim finally lost him in the tangled bushes along the river. There was no doubt in his mind who the thief was. He was the robber who had vanished from Uniontown and whose hideaway he and Danny had found on Saturday in the deep woods beyond Redstone Creek.

Jim leaned up against a tree to catch his breath and think what to do next. His mind worked with lightning speed, and by the time he could breathe normally again it was made up. He knew what he had to do. His father was off on a preaching mission with another minister. They had left that morning in the man's buggy for a nearby village. There was no use talking to Elizabeth; she would be no good in such a situation. He couldn't bear to ask Seph for help. No, he would do it himself, with Danny's help if Danny were willing, or he would do it alone if it were necessary.

He sped back up the hill, skirted the house, rushed into the stable, and flung the saddle on Spartan. In a moment he had the surprised horse out of the stable. He walked him quietly past the parsonage and into the street. As soon as he was out of earshot, he urged the horse to a lively canter and finally to a headlong gallop when they were out in open country. It was almost dark now, but fortunately the clouds had scattered and a full moon was climbing the sky.

Jim was sure that Spartan had never covered the distance

between Brownsville and Redstone Creek in such a short time before. It seemed only a moment until they were pulling up at the Higgins's cabin. By some miraculous good luck, Danny was just coming out the door as Jim arrived. Jim dismounted, and grabbed Danny; holding his hand over his mouth to muffle the shout of surprise. Hurriedly, in whispers, Jim told his story.

"We have to go in after my money, *now!*" Jim finished. "Come on, Dan, right away." As he spoke, he tied Spartan in a place where he could not be seen from the house.

"Oh, no," protested Danny, backing away from Jim's determined grasp. "Oh, no, I'm not agoing into the woods at night, not with that robber loose in there. Not me!"

"We have to go at night, so we won't be seen," said Jim, starting toward the trees. "I'll go alone then, Dan, but I'm going now."

"Wait, Jim," Danny quavered, "wait a minute. I guess I'll go with you."

He caught up with Jim, and the boys vanished into the shadow of the woods, never once thinking, in their intense excitement, that they should have called Danny's father or Mr. Sharpless to go with them. In fact, Jim's planning hadn't gone much further than getting himself out to Danny's as fast as possible. He really had no idea what he would do to get his money back once he got into the woods and came face to face with the thief who had taken it.

"What're you going to do, Jim?" Danny wanted to know as they pushed their way through the undergrowth, guided by the moon and the broken branches from their last trek that way. "We can't fight him. We aren't big enough."

"That's right," agreed Jim, although he felt as strong as two men at the moment. "I guess we'll have to trick him some way. Wonder if he's back yet?"

The time it took to push through to the little clearing seemed endless, but they finally saw it ahead in the moonlight. There was no light in the cabin and no sound. The boys settled themselves where they had first hidden two days before and prepared to wait. For the first time Jim had a chance to think over their situation and realize their danger. Now he began to wish, too late, that he had talked to Seph and told Danny's father what they intended to do. Maybe they would be missed and someone would come to look for them. Maybe someone would see Spartan at Danny's. He hoped so.

It wasn't long before they heard sounds in the woods, something pushing through the undergrowth on the opposite side of the clearing.

"Probably a deer," suggested Danny.

"Naw," whispered Jim, "deer don't talk."

Danny's deer undeniably was talking; red hot words came hurtling through the night as somebody crashed through the thicket surrounding the little hut and fell over a log. The boys shrank back as far as they could into the shadows and hung on to each other. Jim could feel Danny trembling, and he wasn't any too steady himself. He strained his eyes to see the big, dark form that lumbered into the clearing. Although he hadn't been able to see the face of the man who had run off with his money, he felt sure that this was the same one. The general shape seemed to be the same, and he moved with the same lurching gait.

The man fumbled at the door and went in. Then Jim and Danny dared to let their breath out in sighs of relief. Apparently the man hadn't sensed their presence. In a moment they could see light through the cracks of the poorly built cabin. Danny nudged Jim.

"Let's go back and git my Pa," he urged. "We can't git your money alone."

"Maybe we'll have to," Jim conceded unwillingly, "but I want to try a plan I have first."

"We can't fight him, Jim," Danny reminded him for the second time. "He's a big feller. He's twice as big as the two of us put together."

"I know it," replied Jim impatiently, "but I've got a plan. Just wait a little until he goes to bed."

Jim was remembering the old tale of Jack and the Beanstalk that Aunt Margaret had told them over and over again. Jack had managed to steal what he wanted from the old giant as he slept. Maybe he, Jim, could stage a modern Jack and the Beanstalk and make off with his small money bag while this giant robber slept. It was worth trying.

It seemed an eternity that he and Danny crouched in the deep shadows of the thicket. They both shivered with excitement and chill. Jim was almost at the point of giving in to Danny's urging that they go back when he saw the light go out in the cabin.

All of Jim's courage surged back. "Let's count slowly to two hundred," he whispered to Danny, "and then I'm going over there to see what's going on."

They began to count, softly and slowly. "One, two three, four, five—" What if the man had the money bag in his pocket, and Jim couldn't find it? "Nine, ten, eleven, twelve—" What if he had bolted the door, and Jim couldn't get in? "Twenty-five, twenty-six, twenty-seven—"

"Two hundred," whispered Danny.

"All right," said Jim, "here I go!"

He slipped out of the darkness into the moonlit clearing, keeping as close to the dark as possible. Stealthily as a cat he made his way to the door of the hut. Before he touched the door, he peered through the cracks between the logs and held up his hand in a signal of "all's well" to Danny. He could see a faint light inside that apparently came from a fire on the hearth. It wouldn't be pitch dark, at least, and he could see to locate the money bag.

Jim tried the door fearfully. It swung open slowly, and he stepped into the tiny room as silently as an Indian. For a moment he stood perfectly still, growing used to the fire-light. He became aware of sound in the room. It was the

deep, regular breathing of someone asleep, and as he listened it deepened into a heavy snore.

Jim located the man lying across a crude bunk at one side of the hut, fully dressed. If the money bag was in his clothes, Jim's cause was lost. He looked around the room in a panic of uncertainty. In the flickering light from the fire he finally saw his fat, black money bag lying on a little table. It was open. Had the robber taken the coins out and hidden them in his clothes? Scarcely daring to breathe, Jim tiptoed across and looked into the bag. The money was there! Probably the man had been counting it and had forgotten to close the bag before he went to sleep.

Jim pulled the strings tight and slipped the bag into his pocket. He took a final look at the snoring thief and inched his way to the door. In a moment he would be across the clearing, and he and Danny would be plunging toward the Higgins's cabin. But just as he closed the door behind him, it slipped out of his hand and banged with a sickening thud in the silence of the night.

Jim heard a muttered exclamation from the cabin and the sound of heavy, booted feet hitting the floor. He shot across the clearing and leaped after Danny, who was already running as fast as the undergrowth would let him. The boys had a fair start because the man did not come immediately. He evidently stopped a minute to look for the money bag, and was probably still groggy with sleep. Jim and Danny had never been more alert. They climbed nimbly over fallen trees and side-stepped hanging vines. They raced around stumps and leaped over mud puddles.

But soon the boys could hear the man tracking after them as they smashed through the woods. They had the advantage because they saved their breath for running; the robber swore steadily as he pursued them. The boys finally felt sure they were gaining. The man seemed to have lost them, for the sound of his heavy body crashing through the woods wasn't so loud. Jim suddenly caught a glimpse of light through the forest, light in the Higgins's cabin. They were safe now. If their legs could just hold them up a few more minutes, they would be telling their tale by the Higgins's fire.

That was the moment that Danny chose to stumble over

a root and dive head first into a huge mud puddle. Then the robber was on their trail again. Jim could hear him coming, panting and cursing, close behind. Danny tried to get to his feet, but he slipped and went down again in the slimy mud. This time he cried out wildly, and the man yelled. He was almost upon them. Jim could see his evil face in the moonlight and almost feel his hot breath as he lunged forward to pounce.

Jim clutched Danny by the coat collar, gave a super-human heave and leaped over the hole at the same time. His momentum carried them both to firm ground just beyond the man's grasp. The forest was open here as it thinned toward the clearing. Jim began to run again, dragging the terrified Danny after him, and this time he shouted for help. Danny joined in with a right good will.

The cabin door flew open and all the Higginses poured out, Mr. Sharpless with them. They came just as the boys, with the robber at their heels, plunged into the clearing.

"Get him!" gasped Jim, pointing to the man, who was turning to flee back into the woods.

They got him, and brought him back, struggling and protesting that he hadn't done anything wrong, that Jim had broken into his cabin and stolen the money. Mr. Sharpless, knowing the story of the money, took one look at the pouch, hitched up his fast black mare, and he and Mr. Higgins drove into town to turn the robber over to the sheriff.

When they returned, several hours later, Jim and Danny, scrubbed and fed, were sitting by the fire, counting Jim's money. They told their story all over again to the two men, as quickly as they could. Then they wanted to hear about the trip to town.

Mr. Sharpless began his story by telling them first how Mr. Higgins had found Jim's horse when he went to look for Danny. Since both boys seemed to be missing, Mr. Higgins had gone to ask Mr. Sharpless to help hunt for them. The two men had checked back at the Higgins's cabin and were about to search the forest when they had heard the boys call.

The boys waited impatiently through this story. They already knew parts of it. And at last Mr. Sharpless came to what they wanted to hear. In town the robber had finally confessed to the Uniontown robberies, and to the theft of the chickens and Bessie's milk. He also admitted that he had stolen Jim's money. He had been lurking in the bushes the night Jim lost it and had likewise decided to look for it as soon as the rain washed the snow off the hill.

Mr. Sharpless put his hand into his pocket and pulled out two shining silver dollars. He tossed them down into Jim's fat black bag.

"Jim," he said, "I offered a reward for catching the thief who was pilfering my chickens and milking my cow. You caught him, and the reward is yours. It was a foolhardy thing to try all alone at your age, but it was brave. It was mighty brave. Here's fifty cents for Danny, too."

A big grin spread over Jim's face. He jumped up and shook Mr. Sharpless' hand. "Thank you, sir!" he cried. "I guess I never would have caught him if I hadn't slammed the door!"

"One more thing," said Mr. Sharpless. "Don't run off like that again. Your mama was near worried to death when we stopped by."

Jim put his hand to his mouth. He had forgotten about home. What would Papa say when he found out?

Mr. Sharpless glanced slyly at Jim. Then he patted him on the back.

"She's not worried any more, boy. She said she would have done the same thing herself. Told me to tell you to stay here overnight, since it's so late. You can ride the horse in before school in the morning."

Jim heaved a sigh of relief. He had his money, and more. And with Elizabeth on his side, surely Papa wouldn't be angry.

11

PAPA'S DECISION

Jim was walking home from the Higgins's cabin one Sabbath morning in the middle of April. Papa was to preach in the Brownsville church that morning, so he wouldn't be coming out to Redstone Creek. April was soft across the silver-gray hills of Pennsylvania as Jim walked along the muddy road toward home. The air was alive with the sound of birds, and wild flowers blossomed in the woods along the road. Suddenly Jim came out on the brow of the hill that overlooked the Monongahela valley and the little town of Brownsville. He stopped to look, as he always did when he came to this lovely place.

This Sabbath morning it was very quiet. It was too early for meeting, so no horses or buggies or walking people disturbed the stillness.

"Guess I'll go the long way home, by the river," thought Jim. "It's early."

He felt unusually gay because it was his twelfth birth-

112

day. He raced down the long hill. When he came to the river he slowed down and picked his way along the muddy path high above the water. To the left, across the shaggy grass of the small churchyard, the red brick walls of the meetinghouse rose through the trees. Jim crossed the churchyard and on a sudden impulse, he went to the door and tried it. It was unlocked, so he went in and crossed the dark entrance hall into the meeting room. The spring sun shone through the small rose window and laid red and blue patterns on the high pulpit. Ever since Jim had first come to Brownsville, that lofty, soaring pulpit, reached by narrow, winding stairs enclosed in oak paneling, had fascinated him. He had longed from the very depths of his heart to mount those steep stairs and gaze down upon the pews as his father did every Sabbath.

Papa would never let him do it, even when all the people had gone home after meeting and Jim was there alone with him.

"You don't play in the house of the Lord, Jim," Papa always said, half in earnest, half in fun.

Jim never dared argue the point, but he felt Papa was most unreasonable. Now here he was, early on his birthday morning, all alone in the meetinghouse, no one due there for some time. What was to hinder his fulfilling this long-time desire and climbing up into that wonderful pulpit? Absolutely nothing. So Jim opened the small swinging door at the back of the pulpit and began to climb up the winding stairs, with a delicious sense of guilt. In a moment he emerged at the top and stood in front of the preacher's desk, gazing down at the rows of empty pews. He sucked in his cheeks in imitation of his father's thin face, and leaned forward, pounding on the pulpit.

"And now, my beloved brethren," he intoned majestically. He went on preaching a profound sermon to his imaginary congregation. He had never had so much fun. He could imagine his mother and Rene and Seph sitting in their accustomed places. He could see all the familiar people who came every Sabbath to hear Papa preach.

Suddenly he realized it must be getting late, perhaps on toward ten o'clock. Soon the pews would be filling up with very real people. He had to get home and dressed for meeting. In a panic, he turned and rushed down the tiny, steep stairs. He leaped down three at a time in his heavy, leather boots and all at once there was a sickening, splintering crash. A step halfway down gave way under his right foot and he sank in almost to his knee. After a moment of shocked quiet, Jim began to pull his foot up gingerly. It hurt unbearably, and he had to stop every few seconds until the pain subsided again.

After a period of tugging, he realized that he was making no headway at all, because the broken board moved up with every tug. The harder he pulled the tighter it held his leg, until he felt as though he were being squeezed in a vise. He tried to pull the whole step loose with his hands,

114

but nothing happened. He twisted and turned as much as he could stand, but the rugged old board held, and there was nothing he could do. He was a prisoner.

Kneeling on the other knee, he considered his awful plight. It must be very close to meeting time now. All he could do was wait and pray that Papa would come early and alone. The leg didn't hurt so much when Jim stayed perfectly still. He felt quite sure it wasn't broken, probably just skinned and bruised. But what in the world would happen if Papa came too late to get him out? What would happen if he were still there when Papa mounted the pulpit steps to deliver his sermon?

It seemed an eternity, but at last Jim heard the door open. Dr. Penney's firm step resounded in the entry. Jim was just about to call out when he realized that his father was not alone. Someone was talking to him. The solemn voice, Jim knew at once, was that of the senior deacon of the church. Jim could not disgrace Papa by revealing himself. He would have to wait all through the endless service!

People began to stream into the meetinghouse. Jim could tell there was going to be a good attendance. That was good, because maybe Papa would be so pleased with the large congregation that he would be milder with Jim.

The service began. Jim could picture his father sitting in the stately, high-backed chair down on the platform. A man with a strong tenor voice lined out the first hymn:

"How firm a foundation, ye saints of the Lord . . ."

Jim looked down at the broken board and had to grin in spite of himself. How firm a foundation, indeed! Papa read the scripture, and then some names had to be voted on for church membership. Jim's heart pounded so it almost choked him. In a minute it would be time for the sermon, and Papa would be climbing to the pulpit.

The deacons took the offering. Jim could hear the coins dropping into the bare plates. Any minute now——Papa dedicated the offering. It was a matter of seconds——his measured steps came across the low platform. The little door at the back of the pulpit swung open, and he was on the first step. Jim gazed wildly up into his father's stunned face. He pointed mutely to the broken board. It seemed to Jim that his father scarcely hesitated in his climb upward. The shock faded from his face, and he stepped expertly over Jim and continued mounting to the pulpit. Jim settled down miserably for the long sermon.

He decided that this was the longest sermon his father had ever preached. On and on went the familiar voice, but at last it came to an end. Dr. Penney raised his hand in benediction over his people and prayed:

"Unto Him who is able to keep you from falling . . ."

Then he descended, stepping neatly over Jim. Jim hardly knew what to think. Much as he wanted to be free, he dreaded the moment when Papa would say goodbye to the last person and come to him.

"Goodbye, George," said Dr. Penney pleasantly. "Tell

Maria we missed her today and we hope the baby is better soon."

Jim listened to George's fading footsteps and then to his father's, coming toward him. Dr. Penney was humming "How Firm a Foundation" softly under his breath as he approached Jim's prison. In a minute he was there, frowning. Jim looked up dumbly and his father stood back and scratched his ear as he surveyed the situation.

"Hmm," he murmured, "I guess I can get you out, but I must confess I don't know quite how to go about it. Should have kept George here. He's a carpenter."

"This will hurt," he said as he stepped on the board with his own foot. It did hurt, and Jim gritted his teeth as his father bore his full weight on the step. At last it began to give, and in a second Jim was free. Dr. Penney helped him out and down onto a pew.

"Now let's see what the damage is," he said calmly.

Jim pulled down his torn black stocking and his father looked at the hurt leg. It was skinned and swelling painfully. A dark, ugly bruise was spreading over it. Dr. Penney felt it carefully and said, "Nothing broken, luckily. Now tell me, James, what in the name of goodness were you doing there?"

Jim told the whole ridiculous story as he limped home. Papa said very little. Much of the time he kept his face turned away from Jim, so it was hard to tell what was going on in his mind.

Elizabeth and Rene and Seph had gone on home long ago. Now as Jim and Papa rounded the corner to the parsonage, the front door flew open and Seph rushed toward them.

"What took you so long?" he cried. "I saw Caleb Jones after meeting. He's going to California, Papa. That means I'll be on the river! I'll be in the pilothouse of the new boat!"

For a moment Jim forgot all about his throbbing leg. Just one thought pushed all others out of his mind. Seph was going on the river! In a few more weeks he would have the money from Mr. Sharpless. That would make more than enough for the trip. He could go! He could go! He looked up into his father's face, and then his heart sank down into the depths of his muddy boots. As Jim's excited black eyes met Papa's grey ones, there was no warm response, only a cool thoughtful question. In one foolish, childish burst of poor judgment Jim had tossed away weeks of good behavior and hard work.

The family had to be told, of course, where Jim had been during meeting, and why. Rene murmured sympathetically over the bruised leg; Elizabeth hurried to find cloths for cold compresses; Clarissa clucked severely. Seph snorted, but had the good sense to hold his tongue. Jim's hearty appetite had failed completely, and not even Elizabeth's most luscious apple pie, baked especially for his birthday, tempted him.

After dinner he had to sit with his foot up on a stool and a cold, drippy compress on his leg while Seph discussed his summer plans with subdued excitement. Jim didn't dare say a word. He dreaded having the trip West brought into the conversation. He certainly wouldn't introduce the subject today! Suddenly Seph broke off his talk about the new boat and turned to Papa.

"When are you leaving?" he asked. "I suppose you'll wait until school is out for Jim."

He leaned over and gave Jim a brotherly whack on the shoulder.

"Congratulations, fellow! Got enough money in the sugar bowl?"

Jim winced and forced himself to look at Papa for the first time since Seph's announcement.

Dr. Penney cleared his throat. "I don't know," he said slowly. "I had thought, up until this morning, that Jim would surely be going with me if you didn't, Seph; but now, I just don't know."

A thick stillness settled over the room. Dull red spread across Jim's face, and he stared miserably at his swollen leg. Rene played noiselessly with her dolls in the corner, and Elizabeth rocked beside the fire with her hands folded in Sabbath quiet on her lap. Jim waited wearily for someone to break the unbearable silence. A voice sounded through the gloom at last. It was Elizabeth, speaking to his father.

"I think he should go," she said.

She rose from her rocker and drew herself up to her full height. "I think he should go, William," she repeated. She spoke as though the children were not there, as though she were alone with her husband.

"He has tried so hard to be good, and has worked so faithfully for his money. He has grown up doing it, too. I don't think it would be right to punish him that way."

Jim couldn't believe his ears. Elizabeth, who was so gentle and so mild, was telling his father what was right and what was wrong. William and Elizabeth faced each other for a long moment, until he turned away before the fire in her blue eyes.

"But it was disobedience, Elizabeth, sheer disobedience. I had forbidden him ever to play there," he said, still speaking as though they were alone. "If you had been in my place when I opened the door to go up into the pulpit! There was Jim, sprawled all over the stairs. I will never know what prevented me from dying of shock right there. What if I had yelled? What if I had stepped on him and fallen headfirst down the stairs myself?"

There was a muffled explosion in back of him, and Dr. Penney whirled around. Seph had clapped his hands over his mouth, but his eyes rolled with laughter. He struggled for control, but it was useless. The laughter spilled over, and he sat helplessly shrieking. Papa glared at him while Jim sat in terror, not knowing whether to laugh or cry.

Suddenly all the wrath died out of Papa's face and his shoulder's began to shake. In a minute he was gasping with laughter himself. Everybody was laughing—even Jim dared join in with his hoarse chuckle.

Papa finally pulled out his big white handkerchief and wiped his eyes.

"All right," he admitted, "it does have its amusing side when you look back on it. I suppose it wasn't so serious a misconduct as it seemed at first. If you watch your step from now until May, Jim, I guess you can go. Mama seems to think you've grown up."

Jim leaped from his chair, the compress flew off, the basin of water beside him upset.

"Yee-ow! I can go!" he shouted.

He hobbled over to the rocker where Elizabeth had settled herself again, and in spite of his aching leg, he knelt awkwardly beside her.

"Thank you, Mama, thank you!" he whispered into her hair. "I never had such a wonderful birthday!"

12

BY BOAT AND TRAIN

The day had come at last. Jim stood on the bank of the Monongahela on a lovely May morning and waited for Uncle Fred's boat to come around the bend. He and Papa had been invited to ride down to Pittsburgh as guests on the new towboat, "James Rees." Seph, in the pilot house as assistant for a fortnight now, could hardly wait to show them what he had already learned about piloting. Jim and his father were ready, standing on the small dock with their luggage piled around them. The hard-earned twenty-five dollars, in a brand new leather purse, were stowed away in Jim's trouser pocket. The purse was a gift from Grandpa Gilbert. When Jim had opened it, he had found a bright new dollar in its depths.

"Can't ever tell when you might be needing just a mite extra," Harry Gilbert explained.

Jim thought privately that if his plans went right he might be needing a good deal extra before he saw Brownsville again. He had slipped into the study, just before it was time to go down to the dock, and once more had taken the little gold nugget from the drawer.

Elizabeth and Rene were with them at the dock, of course, and Clarissa without her apron was there, too. All of the Higginses and some of the Sharpless family had come in from Redstone Creek. Danny was very silent and his regular grin was missing. Jim understood why.

There was the wail of the whistle, echoing over the soft blue hills. Everybody surged close to the edge to catch the first glimpse of the "James Rees." Jonathan Binns was waiting in his small skiff to row the passengers out to the boat. Jim snatched up his heavy bag; it was time to say goodbye.

"All aboard!" bellowed Jonathan Binns.

Jim gave Rene a hasty peck on the cheek, and turned to Elizabeth. He put out his hand awkwardly to shake hers, but suddenly, in spite of his twelve years and all the people watching, he dropped his bag and threw his arms around her. What if he didn't see her again? He could tell by the tight look around her mouth that she was near tears. He thought he couldn't stand it if she cried. She didn't. She swallowed hard and smiled as she gave him a push toward the boat.

The "James Rees" rounded the bend and steamed majestically toward them, pushing a string of three coal barges. Seph was at the wheel. Jim gave Danny a farewell whack

on the back and jumped into the skiff. Papa followed, and
Jonathan Binns pulled on the oars. The little skiff grazed
the side of the big towboat gently. The travelers climbed
up the swaying rope ladder, and Uncle Fred helped them
onto the deck.

Now they were away on the river. The whistle blew
furiously; everyone shouted good-byes; handkerchiefs
fluttered on shore until Brownsville was lost to sight
around the next bend. Jim raced through the clean, new
boat and up to the pilot house. Seph was steering carefully
downstream, but he grinned at his brother over his shoulder and said, "Hello. The pilot's down having a bite to eat.
Come on in, but don't talk to me."

"I won't," promised Jim, and he stepped reverently inside the glassed-in pilot house.

He had ridden down to McKeesport on the deck of a little stern-wheeler many times, but never had he ridden on a beautiful white towboat, with mighty side-wheels churning the green water.

The trip down to McKeesport, where many of their relatives lived, had never seemed so short. There was no time to stop, but the family was all there to wave them on their way as the towboat steamed by.

Jim had never been as far as Pittsburgh before. It was there that the journey down the great Ohio would begin. The pilot took Seph's place long before they arrived. He edged the towboat gently into the wharf where her barges would be unloaded before the trip back upriver to the West Virginia coal fields.

"There!" exclaimed Dr. Penney, pointing to a great white steamboat tied up near them. "That's the 'Pennsylvania,' Jim. She sails tomorrow morning at six o'clock, and we'll be on board!"

The next morning at six o'clock Papa and Jim were on board, indeed, but the promised sailing did not take place.

"Thought you advertised to leave at six o'clock," Dr. Penney teased the first mate.

"We did," agreed the man, "but we had no idea there would be all these passengers."

He waved his arm toward the stream of men, women,

and children toiling up the gangplank, all struggling with enormous burdens of luggage.

"Are they all going West?" cried Jim.

"Far West," nodded the officer. "They'll go to St. Louis, Missouri, with us, and then they'll hit the trail in wagons, headed for California or Oregon."

"Most of them after gold, I presume," observed Dr. Penney.

"Gold, and homesteads," the mate agreed.

> "I'm going to California,
> The gold dust for to see."

A boy about Jim's age, bending under a mountain of luggage, sang the rollicking tune as he followed his family up the gangplank. Jim nudged his father.

"Don't you wish Mama and Seph and Rene were here and we were all going to the far West, too?"

Dr. Penney laughed. "I do indeed wish your mother were here," he said, "but as for going out to California for gold, I must say Burlington, Iowa, will be far enough for me."

Jim sighed and held his tongue. He jiggled the nugget gently in his pocket.

Wednesday morning, two days behind schedule, the "Pennsylvania" moved away from the noisy, crowded wharf. Jim stood at the jammed rail and watched the city fade into the mist. Papa had met a minister who was going to St. Louis. They were deep in conversation, so Jim went off on his own to explore the big ship.

He had never seen anything so grand as the red-carpeted saloon in the middle of the ship, with its plush furniture and elegant silk wall-hangings. It was crowded with people, as was every other inch of the boat. Jim picked his way carefully, trying to avoid bumping into the huge hoopskirts of the women and girls. There wasn't a breath of fresh air in the room, and soon it seemed unbearably stuffy to him, so he went back on deck.

There people were milling about, trying to find comfortable spots to settle down. Babies were crying in their mothers' arms, and little children whined and whimpered at their skirts. Dr. Penney had finished talking with the minister and had just had an interesting conversation with the captain.

"He tells me," Papa said, as they picked their way through the crowds to their stateroom, "that there are one-hundred-fifty deck passengers on board, all crowded on deck behind the engine. I'd suffocate there in twenty-four hours. We were certainly lucky to get a stateroom, even though it costs more."

"Where are all these people going to sleep at night?" Jim asked.

They were in their tiny, stuffy stateroom now. Jim threw himself on a bunk and watched his father pour water from a big white pitcher to wash his hands.

"Where will they sleep?" Jim repeated.

Dr. Penney wiped his hands. "They'll sleep in the open, Jim, all over the decks and the floor in the cabin. You just wait. Tonight you won't be able to step for the people. It's all right as long as the good weather holds and there's no sickness."

In the early evening Jim rushed back to the deck to watch fascinated, while mothers put their tired children to bed on folded quilts or feather pillows. One family had managed to stake out a spot large enough to spread a feather bed, and all five of their children were curled up on it like a litter of puppies.

Sunset had begun to stain the waters of the shining river green and rose and purple. The splash of the great paddle wheels seemed to hush, and the throb of the engine quieted. Jim noticed that the people had quieted, too, with the coming of evening. The babble of talk that had gone on all day was stilled.

Dr. Penney was inside, using the last bit of fading light to start a letter to Elizabeth. Jim made up his mind to go in, too. It was dull outside, with everybody settling down for the night and many people already snoring in their blankets.

Suddenly the "Pennsylvania" swung around a great sweeping curve in the river, and Jim saw a town ahead in the twilight.

"Parkersburg!" somebody yelled.

The engine was cut, and the "Pennsylvania" glided toward the shore. The last rays of the setting sun fell upon the wharf, and Jim could see that it was full of people and horses. All the passengers on the boat except the sleeping children were soon up, crowding to the rail to see what was happening.

Jim pushed through the crowd to the door of their stateroom and called excitedly, "Papa, come quick! We're at Parkersburg and a lot of people are getting on."

Dr. Penney dropped his letter and came out on deck. Jim managed to wriggle his way up to the rail where he could see everything. Close to the edge of the dock stood a small group of elegantly dressed white people, surrounded by luggage. In back of them, and entirely covering the rest of the wharf were at least a hundred Negroes. Jim whirled and looked up into his father's face. His black eyes were full of unspoken questions.

Dr. Penney nodded and formed the word silently with his lips, "Slaves."

The gangplank was down and the white family boarded the "Pennsylvania." Next, twenty beautiful, high-spirited horses were led across and taken down to the hold. Last of all, the hundred slaves were driven onto the boat. They are treated just like the horses, Jim thought, as they were sent up to the top deck which they covered completely.

Jim watched them go past, each with his little bundle on his shoulder, and listened to the snarling voice of the overseer goading on the stragglers. He stood close to his father, and for the first time in his life he was speechless. It was not the first time he had seen Negroes, by any means. In fact, several times there had been one or two "people of color" who had settled in their neighborhood and been members of Dr. Penney's church. But those people were free Negroes. This was the first time he had seen slaves.

Jim was just about to speak when the captain loomed up in the dusk.

"Good evening," he greeted them. "Having a pleasant trip in spite of the crowds?"

"Yes, indeed," Papa responded politely. "This is my son, James, Captain."

Jim felt honored beyond words to have his hand shaken by the captain.

"Did you know ahead of time, sir, that all those people were going to get on at Parkersburg?" Jim asked.

The captain chuckled. "Yes. I knew they'd be with us this trip. They came from Old Virginia, and they are going to live on a new plantation in Kentucky. We certainly didn't need them to make a crowd, did we?"

"We certainly didn't," nodded Dr. Penney. "By the way, Captain, is there any sickness on the boat that you know of? Crowded conditions like these spread sickness like wildfire."

The captain's cheerful face clouded. "I know," he said, "that's the thing we dread most on the river—even more than explosions. Let just one person get sick on a crowded boat, and it spreads all over in a few hours, seems as though. We're lucky so far this trip, not a trace of sickness."

Dr. Penney looked thoughtful. "What do you hear from downriver, Captain?"

"Well," said the captain reluctantly, "I did hear a rumor of a bit of cholera below, but we don't need to worry. We'll steer clear of that."

"Hmm," murmured the doctor. "Goodnight, Captain. It was good to talk with you. I think we'll turn in. It's been a pretty big day for us."

Jim was quiet until they had stepped over dozens of sleeping forms and wedged themselves into their own stateroom. Then he said excitedly, "My, if there should be cholera on the boat, isn't it lucky you'll be here to take care of folks?"

Dr. Penney snorted. "If there is cholera on the boat, and it will be a miracle if there isn't, it will spead like fire in the forest. All the doctors in the world wouldn't be able to stop it. I think we'll get off the boat at Cincinnati, Jim."

"Oh," wailed Jim, "we just got on, and you said we'd go to St. Louis."

"I know I did, Jim," his father replied, "but I didn't know then that there would be such crowds on the boat. I don't like the sound of this cholera rumor. Once cholera is started, it runs like a mad dog and there's no known remedy for it."

Jim bit his tongue to hold back the torrent of disappointed words.

"I don't think this trip's going to be much fun if we're going to be scared of every little thing," he said finally.

Papa's eyes began to twinkle. "I wouldn't exactly call a possible cholera epidemic a little thing," he said mildly, "and I'm sorry to spoil your boat trip. But I thought maybe you might enjoy a ride on the train from Cincinnati up to Sandusky."

It took Jim a few seconds to absorb what his father had just proposed and then he whooped, "The train! I've never been on a train in my life. We can ride on a boat any old time at home. Let's get off and take the train!"

13

DOCTOR JIM

Early the next morning, Jim and Dr. Penney were watching dawn break over southern Ohio from the dirty windows of a railroad coach. Jim flattened his nose against the pane and watched the country plunge past. It seemed as if they were flying. By evening they would be at Sandusky, two hundred-fifty miles away!

Jim, used to the soft, blue, sheltering hills of Western Pennsylvania, was astonished at the great flat land that stretched away to the horizon on every side.

"Do you like it without hills?" he asked his father.

Dr. Penney laughed. "I don't know yet, Jim. It's certainly easier to get around here. We'll be seeing a lot of new country before we get back home again."

Jim nodded, and his hand sought the silver dollar and the cool little nugget of gold, nested in his pocket.

In the evening the train whistled its way into the town of Sandusky, on the shores of Lake Erie. Jim was too tired even to enjoy the excitement of the hotel where they ate a late supper and crawled into bed.

The lake boat that they boarded in the morning wasn't much different from the river boats Jim was used to seeing at home. But the trip across the end of Lake Erie up to Detroit was completely different. For most of the six hours they were out of sight of land. All they could see was the sparkling blue of the lake, stretching off to the edge of the sky in every direction. Jim spent most of his time dreaming at the rail. It was easy to imagine they were on the ocean, sailing around the Horn for California.

"Maybe I won't go home again," he whispered to himself, boldly. "Maybe I won't."

"Detroit, Jim!" called his father, and Jim jerked out of his reverie to see the low skyline of Detroit rising ahead of them.

The next morning, early, they were on the train again, chugging across the state of Michigan. At New Buffalo, on the shore of Lake Michigan, they found the steamer waiting that would take them to Chicago.

"They tell me," said Dr. Penney, "that it takes only a few hours to run up to Chicago. What an age of miracles we live in!"

He was walking briskly up the gangplank of the steamer as he spoke. Jim, lugging his heavy bag, sighed. Papa didn't seem at all tired by the traveling. Perhaps it was because he was accustomed to journeying on horseback hundreds of weary miles along forest trails in Pennsylvania. The boats and trains must seem very comfortable by comparison. Jim was tired, very tired. Exciting as it was to sail on the great steamboats or ride in the trains, his muscles cried out for a run beside his river or a climb in the soft, green hills.

The sun was setting behind a pile of threatening black clouds, as the steamer prepared to set out.

"I certainly hope we don't have a storm on the way up," said Dr. Penney, as he stowed his luggage away in their stateroom. "I'm not a very good sailor in rough weather."

Jim privately thought it would be kind of fun. Lake Michigan was so vast that it would be real adventure, just like a storm at sea.

"I don't know whether I'm a good sailor or not," he replied. "I've never had a chance to find out."

"If the lake starts to roll, you'll soon know," said his father grimly. "I'm afraid this warm day has been a weather breeder."

The lake was glassy smooth as the boat's engines started and the great paddle wheel began to turn. They moved out of the harbor, away from the village of New Buffalo, with the music of the whistle echoing across the water. Early darkness settled oppressively around the big steamer. The shore was hidden abruptly, and they seemed to be muffled in the clouds that had blotted out the sun.

"We had better get some rest," said Dr. Penney, "but

I don't think that we ought to undress. With any luck at all, we should be in Chicago before midnight."

He hung his shabby black coat carefully on a hook, loosened his cravat, and stretched out on the lower bunk.

"D'you mind if I go out for awhile and stretch my legs?" Jim asked.

"Not at all," yawned his father. "Just don't fall overboard."

Jim stepped out into the darkness. There were a few lanterns burning on deck, but their small light did little to illuminate the night. He felt his way to the rail and looked over. The water, so far below, glittered as black as the coal that drifted down the Monongahela on the barges. Its mirror surface was shattered now by choppy waves, and he could hear the wind rising. No one else had ventured out on deck. He was alone in the night.

Suddenly Jim felt uneasy. He shivered in the chill of the wind and turned back toward the cabin. Before he had reached the door to their stateroom, the unnatural stillness was ripped by a sound that sent his heart into his mouth. It was an explosion—small and muffled, but definitely an explosion of some kind—and it was followed by shouts and commotion.

The boiler couldn't have blown up, he thought wildly. Jim had seen a steamboat explode on the Monongahela once, and he had never forgotten the mighty roar of that explosion. This one was too small to be the boiler. He

137

started to run toward the sound. Papa had heard and came rushing from the stateroom. Other doors flew open, and passengers poured out on deck.

There was the sound of pounding footsteps and someone yelled, "Is there a doctor on board?"

"Here!" shouted Dr. Penney. "Get my bag, Jim. Quick!"

Jim didn't need urging. He leaped into the stateroom and plunged out seconds later with the worn black bag in his hand. He caught up with his father on the ladder down to the engine room. Someone below was holding a lantern for them to see.

"What happened?" Jim demanded.

"Blew the head out of the cylinder," replied the crew-man briefly. "No great damage done, but one of the boys got caught. Like to tore his arm right off, looks like. He's bleedin' bad, Doc."

Jim jumped down from the third rung of the ladder and followed his father to the little crowd of men in the engine room. The captain was bending over the injured sailor, who lay on the floor. A little, bright pool of blood widened under his shoulder.

The men moved back and stood in respectful silence. Dr. Penney spoke reassuringly to the man and stooped quickly to feel for his pulse.

"That's good, it's full and bounding," he said in relief.

"Put him on the table there. Have to cut this sleeve away first, so I can see what I'm doing and get the bleeding stopped."

The sailors lifted the wounded man onto a table and the doctor, as gently as he could, ripped the sleeve off with his pocket knife and revealed the wound. It was bleeding heavily, and the man's face was yellow-white in the flickering lantern light. Dr. Penney examined the entire wound carefully.

"Hmm—not as bad as I feared. Fortunately, no bones broken, but a couple of small arteries were cut. That's what makes it look so bad. It's deep, though, and it'll need stitches, once we get this bleeding stopped."

Papa looked at Jim and went on softly, "Good thing you're here to help, Jim."

Jim gulped. He could feel his face going white. He tried to turn his eyes away, but he was curiously fascinated. He had never been with his father when he was taking care of an injury. Now he found he couldn't pull his gaze away from the thin, grave face, so intent on the injured arm. Dr. Penney was working rapidly. He fashioned a tourniquet from bandages in his bag and deftly twisted it around the arm above the wound.

"Hold this snug," he directed Jim.

Jim obeyed, and in a few seconds the flow of blood dwindled and stopped.

"Good." The doctor nodded. "Now we'll have to clamp

140

these two small arteries that were cut. Somebody get me some soap and water. Hand me the forceps, Jim."

He took the instrument from Jim, quickly washed it, and used it to get hold of the severed ends of the arteries.

"Clamps," he said crisply.

Jim found them in the bag and washed them carefully, as he had seen his father do with the forceps. Dr. Penney clamped the arteries so the bleeding was cut off effectively, and then he expertly packed the wound.

"Now," he said comfortably, "We'll just wait awhile until we're sure this bleeding isn't going to start up again."

He took his big silver watch out of his pocket and handed it to Jim.

"You keep track for me, Jim. We must wait seven minutes."

While Jim watched the slow minutes tick away, Dr. Penney was preparing to sew up the wound. He washed the needle with soap and water, and then gently swabbed the area around the injury.

"Seven minutes—time's up," announced Jim.

"All right, Jim. Now you stand by to help when I need you."

Once more Jim felt he couldn't bear to watch, but neither could he bear not to. He was torn between his admiration for the sure, skillful movements of the doctor's long fingers, and the bulldog grit of the wounded man.

"There!" Dr. Penney murmured in satisfaction. He had

removed the clamps and drawn the jagged edges of the wound firmly together, sewing them snugly in place. Jim handed him bandages from his bag and watched him wrap the arm securely. Dr. Penney straightened his aching back and pulled down his sleeves.

"Now, put him on a cot. I don't want him in a hammock. He should be all right, but he's lost a lot of blood. I'll sit up with him tonight. Feel better about him if I do. I'll be back in a few minutes."

Jim and Papa climbed back up the ladder and walked along toward their stateroom. The anchor had been dropped when the engine was disabled, and the big boat began to roll quite noticeably. Lake Michigan foamed with great racing whitecaps that flashed silvery-white in the lightning. The threatening clouds had spilled their storm at last.

"Going to have a little blow, looks like," said the genial voice of the captain behind them. "Hope you're a good sailor, Doctor."

Papa swallowed uncomfortably. "Not too good a one, I'm afraid," he answered with a feeble grin. "I don't suppose there's a chance we can get to Chicago tonight?"

"My, no," said the captain. "We'll just have to ride her out. Won't be too bad. In the morning there'll be a boat along that can tow us up to Chicago. You folks going far?"

"Up to Rockford," Dr. Penney said hastily. "Relatives of my wife there."

"Mighty lucky thing for my man that you were on board tonight," the captain went on. "Chances are he'd have bled to death or at least lost his arm if you hadn't been. Fine assistant you have here!" He patted Jim's shoulder. "You going to be a doctor like your papa, Son?"

The familiar, quick "NO!" rose to Jim's lips, but he didn't say it this time. Instead, he stood unaccountably silent in the stormy night. His father answered for him.

"He really doesn't know yet what he wants to do, Captain. Lots of time to decide. Come on, Jim. I want to get back to my patient. Goodnight, sir."

There was a strange urgency in Papa's voice. Jim looked at him quickly. In a flash of lightning Dr. Penney looked extremely pale. His face had a queer, greenish cast. They hurried along to their stateroom. Once safely inside, Papa sank weakly onto his berth and groaned.

Jim bent over him in alarm. "What's the matter?" he begged. "What happened?"

Papa moaned again. "It's the boat—this awful rolling. I told you I was a bad sailor, Jim. I didn't take long to show you, did I?" He gave a sickly grin, and struggled to get to his feet.

"Maybe I'll be better in a few minutes. I've got to go and watch that sailor. A doctor can't be sick."

"You just lie here and rest," ordered Jim. "I'll take care of the sailor."

Papa, who was always so brisk and capable, looked up at

him pathetically. "Aren't you the least bit seasick?" he asked. "I can't see why I am, and you aren't."

Jim laughed. "I never felt better in my life," he assured his father. "Tell me what to do, and I'll keep watch for you."

Dr. Penney made one more attempt to stand, and then he sank back and gave Jim orders. Jim went off to find the sailor and begin his long vigil.

He sat down beside the cot and looked at his patient. The man's face had a better color, and he was sleeping. Now it was up to Jim to keep himself awake. The roll of the steamer that made Dr. Penney so ill only rocked Jim like a cradle. The wind sighing around the portholes was a lullaby.

He had borrowed his father's big silver watch. Now he took it from his pocket and looked at it in the faint light from the lantern. It was almost midnight. Jim sighed and began to sing to himself. First he tried the few Stephen Foster songs he knew. As he sang "O Susanna," he was reminded of the words Danny had taught him:

"I'm going to California,
The gold dust for to see"

He jingled the dollar and the nugget vigorously in his pocket and let his mind wander off to the West in the old familiar way. He waited for the magic to work. Never before had he failed to feel the lift of adventure and ex-

144

citement when he thought of California. Tonight nothing happened at all. Instead, he found himself wondering if the sailor sleeping before him would have exchanged all the gold in California for Dr. Penney's skill and care.

The long night wore on. The patient moaned in his sleep. Jim hoped the man wouldn't wake up, but he did. His eyes, full of pain, fastened trustingly on Jim. For a panicky moment he thought of rushing off to get his father, but he remembered the sickly green of Dr. Penney's face. It was all up to him, now, he knew. Jim straightened his shoulders and recalled Papa's instructions. He turned the sailor's hot pillow and gave him a drink of water. He bathed his hot forehead. The man sighed gratefully and closed his eyes again.

The hours were slowly ticking away on Papa's big silver watch. It was almost three o'clock when the sailor moaned again. Jim gave him more water, and he went back to sleep. The next time Jim caught himself dozing he stood up and walked around for a few minutes. This was the first time in his life that he could remember having to stay awake all night. Once he remembered he had roused in the middle of the night to hear his father's weary feet climb the parsonage stairs. He had heard Elizabeth say, "You're so tired, William. Did you have to stay so long?"

His father had answered, "Yes, I had to stay. He needed me."

Jim had rolled over and been glad he wasn't the one who had to sit up all night with a sick man. Now he *was* the one. He knew he would never forget the expression in the wounded sailor's eyes when he gave him a drink of water. For the first time he began to understand what kept his father going.

Along toward dawn when silver light began to filter through the porthole, Jim was aware of the captain's standing behind him.

"You've done well, lad," he said. "How did you ever manage to stay awake?"

Jim's only answer was a grin. He couldn't have put into words, at least not to the captain, what had been going through his mind.

He noticed that the lake had quieted and the wind had

gone down. The boat was riding quite calmly at anchor, and he heard his father's step. Dr. Penney looked pale and worn, but the awful green color had disappeared from his face, and he was smiling.

"Well, Jim!" he said, "I see you're still awake. Good work, boy. How's our patient?"

He looked intently at the sailor and put his hand on his forehead.

"Hmm," he murmured. "He looks all right, and there's no fever. A few days' rest should fix him up. Don't let him use that arm for a while. Come on, Jim. You need some sleep before we get to Chicago."

The captain put his arm across Jim's shoulder as he rose to go with his father.

"Thank you, Jim," he said. "It's plain to be seen you're your father's own son!"

14

JIM'S DECISION

"Everybody out!" bellowed the stage driver. Jim was delighted to get out of the wagon and stretch his legs, even though it meant climbing down into the oozy black mud of the Illinois prairie.

"Watch out, Jim!" called his father.

The warning came too late. Jim landed in a puddle over his boot tops, and went squishing around looking for the road that was practically lost under pools of muddy water.

"Had plenty of rain around these parts lately," drawled the driver, guiding his horses around Jim's puddle. "Makes the road bad."

"What road?" Jim whispered to his father. They smothered their laughter.

They were riding up to Rockford from Chicago in a country wagon with a linen cover over it, and it had rained almost all the way. Now the dark was falling, cold and wet and dismal. It wasn't so bad, unloading the stage in the daylight when they could see where they were going, but at night the only way they could find the mudhole the stage driver was trying to avoid was to fall into it. Everybody was tired, shivering, and very damp after a day of climbing in and out of the wagon and tramping through bogs.

"Tell you what," suggested the driver, dismounting from his high seat and coming up to his miserable passengers, "There's a little town name of Marengo just over the rise there. Thought maybe you'd like to stop and get a bite of warm supper and dry off a little."

A cheer went up from the group. In a few more minutes they were all tramping into the inn where it was warm and dry.

After a good hot meal, Jim was feeling revived and very anxious to get on to Rockford and Aunt Ellen's house. The rest of the trip wasn't quite so uncomfortable. They still had to scramble out of the stage and walk when they came to low, wet ground, but the cold rain had stopped, and the moon had come out to light their way. It was noon the next day when they finally reached Rockford and found their way to Aunt Ellen Peters' house.

Uncle Peters, Aunt Ellen, and their daughter, Eliza, were waiting. Aunt Ellen had swept and scrubbed and polished the guest room until everything glistened. She and Eliza had been cooking for days in preparation for their coming. There was fresh bread and cake, and pies, and everything hungry travelers, long from home, could want. They were tired travelers, too, so when Uncle Peters and Aunt Ellen coaxed them to stay for several days, they were glad to accept.

Jim polished his muddy boots, and Aunt Ellen sponged and pressed his rumpled clothes. He looked fairly presentable the next morning, which was the Sabbath, when he went off to meeting with Papa and the rest of the family. In the afternoon Papa preached in the Rockford church, and Jim listened to him with great pride. For the first time that he could remember, he was glad that it was the Sabbath and glad that he could go to meeting and hear his father preach. It gave him a chance to think quietly and without interruption about many of the things that had been filling his mind since his experience on the boat.

Later they all sat around in Aunt Ellen's parlor and talked while Dr. Penney began a letter to Elizabeth:

My dear Elizabeth:

Seated in your aunt's parlor in the best of health and spirits, I take my pen to write to you—

"Tell her about the man who got hurt on the boat," interrupted Jim, "and that you were seasick and I wasn't, and about wading through the mud on the way up from Chicago."

"I will," Papa promised, writing rapidly.

"Tell her it would be just perfect if only she were here,

150

too," reminded Aunt Ellen. "We wish for her every hour."

"Indeed we do!" Papa agreed wholeheartedly, as he scribbled that down.

"Tell her," broke in Uncle Peters, "that she may not get her boy back. We need a boy in this family, and I'm planning to keep him here."

"You may not get——" wrote Papa, absent-mindedly, and then suddenly he stopped.

"Now what are you talking about, Peters!" he exclaimed, laughing. "That was a close call. I almost put that in the letter."

"Meant for you to put it in the letter," boomed Uncle Peters. "We've needed a brother for Eliza these many years."

He turned to Jim, who was staring at him openmouthed.

"Aren't you the young fellow who's been so all-fired bent on going West? Sure as anything, I remember your mama wrote you were eating your heart out for adventure —wanted to go to California after gold."

"Well, yes, I was," gasped Jim, "but——"

"This isn't California," went on Uncle Peters, "but it's a sight closer to it than Pennsylvania."

His eyes were twinkling, but Aunt Ellen said seriously, "I'm sure he does mean what he says, Jim. Ever since he set eyes on you yesterday, he's been yearning to keep you. You're just the kind of boy he's always wanted."

The twinkle was gone from Uncle Peter's eyes. He

leaned forward and spoke to Jim in a very earnest voice.

"Boy," he said, "I'd raise you just like my own son; give you everything I could. This is still pioneer country out here, you know; lots of adventure in the Rock River Valley for a youngster. Later on you could go farther West if you wanted to."

He turned to Dr. Penney, "William, you've got another boy at home, and you and Elizabeth will have more, like as not. Can't you spare this one to us for a few years at least?"

Dr. Penney was sitting perfectly still, with his dark grey eyes fixed on Jim's face. There was no laughter in them now. At last he shifted in his chair and looked at Uncle Peters.

"This is a decision that Jim will have to make," he said slowly, and to Jim the words seemed to echo and re-echo in the quiet room. "It is a very important decision, but I think he is old enough to make it for himself. However, he must have time to think about it."

Everybody looked at Jim. The beat of his heart seemed to slow and deepen. It sent the hot blood surging up into his face. This was the invitation he had dreamed of for so long. It was just as he had planned it. Suddenly he sprang to his feet and faced his father. He spoke directly to him, and it was as though they were alone. Unconsciously he put his hand into his pocket, and it came out with the little gold nugget clasped tightly in it.

"I don't need time, Papa," he said. "My decision is made already. I think I made it on the boat when the sailor got hurt. I don't want to go to California. This probably seems strange to you, because I haven't had time to talk to you about it since I decided. Maybe I *am* going to be the one in the family to be a doctor. Mama said she thought so. I don't know yet, for sure, but I do know that I'm going home."

He turned the little gold nugget over in his hand, and then he held it out to his father.

"Here," he said, "you take this, and this time you keep it. I won't be wanting it again until I need it for schooling. I'm sure I'm going to want it for that some day. I've made up my mind."

Dr. Penney took the bit of gold in his hand. He looked at it thoughtfully for a moment and then slipped it into the pocket of his worn black coat. His eyes lit up and he put his arm around Jim's shoulders.

"Very well, son," he said, "we'll take it home and you, too. Nothing could please me more!"

Jim turned and looked at Uncle Peters and Aunt Ellen.

"Thank you very much, sir," he said gravely to Uncle Peters. "It would be fine to stay here with you, but I think you can see that I *must* go home."

Papa and Jim did go home. It took quite a long time to

get there, because they went across the state of Illinois to the mighty Mississippi and down to Burlington. There they visited Penneys who had migrated to Iowa, and explored part of the state on horseback. Jim had never been so happy in his life. It seemed to him that an unbearable burden had rolled off his shoulders and he could enjoy every minute of the journey.

Then began the long unwinding——back across Illinois to Chicago, down the lake, no storm, no accident this time, back across Michigan and Ohio to the river, the long, placid hours on the boat, steaming East to Pittsburgh, no crowds going in this direction.

Jim stood on the deck of the little stern-wheeler, chugging up to Brownsville on the Monongahela. The soft hills of Pennsylvania folded him about. Blue twilight covered the familiar land. One more curve in the river and the little town lay spread out in the valley, drowsing at the end of the warm June day. The long eerie call of the steamer sounded against the hills. Jim strained his eyes to see ahead. There was the boat coming out from the wharf to pick them up. It was Jonathan Binns in his little skiff.

They were drawing nearer now; he could see motion on the shore. A bright spot glowed suddenly through the dusk. It was Danny, Danny Higgins and his red head! He heard a squeal above the noise of the engine, and saw a flutter of white. That was Rene. The ladder was over the side; they were in the skiff. Jonathan Binns was talking to them, Papa was responding, but Jim couldn't remember even speaking to him.

His eyes were searching, past Danny, past Rene, up the path from the wharf. Elizabeth was coming. She had heard the whistle. She was running down the path, her long skirts gathered up in her hands. Now she was on the wharf and her arms were open wide. Jim made a flying leap across a strip of green water, and her arms gathered him in.

"I'm home, Mama!" he cried. "I came back home, and I'm going to stay."

AUTHOR'S NOTE

Jim Penney was a real boy, and the background of the story is true. All of the main characters were members of my own family who lived more than a hundred years ago in western Pennsylvania. Elizabeth did marry Dr. Penney. She mothered Seph and Jim and Rene, and after a few years there were three more children in the family, the youngest of whom was my grandmother, Josephine.

We gathered the material for the book from old letters, and newspaper clippings, and the ancient minute books in churches where Great-grandfather Penney used to be minister. When I was almost ready to begin writing, my family and I went to Pennsylvania for a vacation. We drove along the green Monongahela where Jim used to play. We followed the narrow, winding road to Redstone Creek, probably the very same one that Dr. Penney took on his way to meeting. The little church is still there.

In Brownsville we found the old red brick church being torn down, but the minister of the present church took us through the warm July twilight to see it.

Dr. Penney did go West in May of 1849. He sailed on the "Pennsylvania." His fascinating letters to Elizabeth told all about the trip. The family with the slaves did come aboard at Parkersburg. He did leave the boat at Cincinnatti and take the train for fear of cholera, and he wrote a most amusing description of his miserable seasickness on the way up Lake Michigan to Chicago. Also, the head did blow out of the cylinder! All of the muddy details of the stage journey to Rockford were true. However, Dr. Penney went alone on this trip West. We thought how much more fun he would have had if Jim had gone along, so in the book we let him go!

Jim grew up to be a doctor, just as Elizabeth thought he would. He was Dr. James Lowry Penney who practiced medicine for many years in and around McKeesport, Pennsylvania.

J

Withbridge

JIM   ''S